NEON NOON

Advance Praise for *Neon Noon*

'An impressive new voice. A whole new way of storytelling. *Neon Noon* is a compelling read. And it is indeed a delight to read Solanki's captivating prose.' – Anees Salim

'*Neon Noon* is a truly accomplished debut. A searing exploration of love, loss, sex and the making of literature. Solanki is staking out new ground for Indian writing in English.' – Kaushik Barua

NEON NOON

TANUJ SOLANKI

FOURTH ESTATE • *New Delhi*

First published in India in 2016 by Fourth Estate
an imprint of HarperCollins *Publishers*

HarperCollins Publishers India, Cyber City, Building 10-A, Gurugram,
Haryana-122002, India
www.harpercollins.co.in
1 2 3 4 5 6 7 8 9 10

P-ISBN: 978-93-5029-694-3
E-ISBN: 978-93-5029-695-0

Typeset in 11/15 Adobe Garamond Pro at SURYA, New Delhi

Printed and bound at
MicroPrints India, New Delhi

HarperCollins Publishers, Macken House, 39/40 Mayor Street
Upper, Dublin 1, D01 C9W8, Ireland

Von einem gewissen punkt an gibt es keine rückkehr mehr. Dieser punkt ist zu erreichen.
(From a certain point on there is no more returning. That point must be reached.)

—Franz Kafka

PART ONE

The Shattered Idyll

I Never Think of Those Two Nights

~ ~ ~ ~

Hi T,

Quite a while, right? Maybe this surprises you. I thought a lot before sending this email.

I've been following your short stories in all those magazines, and the news is that we are competitors now, for I too have written a short story. I want you to read it. It doesn't have a title as of now, but maybe you can help me with that.

If you read it (and I hope you read it), you'll see how I took some liberties with the timing, the exact actions, so on.

Tell me what you think about it? But if you think it's better not to write back, don't write back. That's okay.

But if you choose to write back, maybe you can also tell me if you've moved houses, if you've changed some things, travelled somewhere, or plan to.

Basically, how are things?

Best,

S

<Untitled>

Two drunken meaningless nights—that's all they were, nothing more.

At that time, December 2012, I was working as a copyeditor for an LGBT publishing house in Mahalaxmi. Rectifying erotica—that was my job. I got the job after a very basic lie. Martha, the edgy chief editor who interviewed me at a loud downtown café, clearly preferred people from what she called 'the community'. I needed the money badly, no full-time opportunities were coming up, and so I told Martha that I was lesbian. She didn't seem to need any other qualification. A week later, I found myself in the firm, piled with so much work that it made me wonder if they had been waiting for me for months. What I had to read was tiresome initially, even irritating, with all those male characters getting intimate with each other, but I took solace in the fact that things had finally started chugging along for me.

I was managing some scribbling of my own too, but those were primarily the days when an alternate realization was gaining a hold on me: that my poems had no ability to suggest what was beyond language, that my poems were imprisoned in their words and in their planar feelings—that they just couldn't and wouldn't do what poetry was really supposed to, whatever that is. My total output until then was a set of forty-one poems, some of which I would send out for publication. I received a steady flow of impersonal rejection letters from the more reputed literary magazines. There were, however, some freak acceptance letters; the most recent one had happened in November, when a short poem found space in the print issue of a highly-thought-of magazine.

It was through that magazine that I knew T. He had been a regular fiction contributor to it. I had read all his stories there, and he seemed interesting. His stories suggested that he was young and struggling with youth, which was a problem I believed I shared with him.

The issue I had been published in also carried one of T's stories. I remember particularly liking that story of his; I think it was called *The Bombay of Life*, and it had something to do with love and literature, and how a writer's life can be a vacillation between the two. It had a sense of vulnerability. I liked that.

Surprisingly for me, T knew me as a poet, which is something I learnt when he accepted my friend request and chatted with me. On chat windows, he used all the right punctuation, never abbreviated, never distended, and always ended sentences with a period. I wanted to meet him in person, and it was not long before I mentioned this to him. He thought it was a good idea. I proposed Janata Bar in Bandra, a place I found comforting since it was inexpensive—something I knew from having frequented it with my university friends. The location also worked for T as he lived close to it, in fact only a hundred or so metres away.

I remember that when I was on the long train ride that evening—toward Bandra station, diddling through a book of poetry that I had recently stolen from a friend—I was thinking about the postures and mannerisms that could suit the evening. I was thinking how I'd already perceived and shaped T's online persona to fit whatever criteria I had at the time, and I had the notion that he had done the same to me. Seduction was a word I had always liked the sound of. But I resolved that I wouldn't sleep with him that night. I had been doing a lot of that those days.

Janata Bar is a place for the janata. The tables are non-exclusive, which is to say you share your table; and therefore the chances of meeting new people are high. The young and/or 'young-at-heart' come to Janata. Once, I remember, I overheard a conversation between three guys well into their fifties. *I don't want to marry her, I just want to fuck her*, one of them said. The others goaded him on. So yes, that's the kind of 'young-at-heart' people who come to Janata. The rest are in their twenties, mostly copyeditors or advertisers or designers who work in Bandra's tiny creative agencies—guys and girls who think of themselves as *cool*, but don't really have the money to go to better, more expensive places. Only the MBA guys get to go to the better places.

T was an MBA guy. As he stepped into Janata, dressed formally after work, lugging a laptop bag on his left side, I had a moment when I thought this could be a mistake. He might not belong here as much as I did. We shook hands in a gesture so formal that it was almost comic. But he settled down quickly, then ordered a quarter of Royal Stag. His brand of whiskey reassured me.

You're quite a writer, I said.

T didn't answer. He just reached for the book in my hand, took it, flipped over a few pages and returned it without reading anything.

How is life, I asked him. I'm reading this book, T said. What book, I asked. Well, I am reading what I call the graveyard writers, he said. He didn't really name the book, I thought. And who would the graveyard writers be, I asked. Roberto Bolaño, Sadat Hasan Manto, T said. I don't know either of them, I said, shrugging. T smiled at that, and I feared I'd conclusively revealed how much of an outsider

I really am to this whole business of literature. It is one thing to write poems, quite another to know the writers other people expect you to know (and you suspect you should).

I love their writing, T said with a flourish of his hands. The spontaneity. Sometimes I feel they create the illusion, the illusion that they are not concerned with the demands of the narrative, that they are just rambling—recording events and conversations. But you can't miss the sense of doom in each sentence. The story always reaches a precipice from where everything is hurled. And down it all comes—all crash and burn.

This guy is a reader, I told myself. Do you read a lot, I asked him.

Wish I could read a little less and write a little more, he said.

I nodded, as if I knew a lot about what he was saying. You must have a big library, I said.

I can't say, he said.

We talked about some other things then. Slowly the whiskey diminished and another quarter was ordered. We got tipsy. We hushed a joke about the two men we were sharing our table with. We joked about the pictures that hung on the walls, especially the one above the cash counter: a naked Jain guru making a gesture akin to catching a basketball for some reason, something that I'd always found funny here at Janata. T never really laughed. The maximum he offered was a smile.

I, finding T generally reticent, started speaking of things I knew about, or thought I knew about. I began by talking about my work at the publishing house. Then I talked about erotica, about the fundamentals of good erotica. I talked about *Venus in India*. At some point I enumerated what I liked about D.H. Lawrence's poetry. I talked about the ripe peaches of Lawrence's poetry, passions on the brink, passions served, the ethic of serving passions.

All through this, T looked at me with a blank expression, lips parted, eyebrows slightly raised. If he was interested, it was only a mild interest, and eventually he did cut me off.

Let's move, let's go to my place, he said. I, being myself, immediately switched into thinking about the possibilities of the night. Yes, let's go, I said, and we were off from Janata Bar in five minutes.

T was not just the MBA guy—he was the *rich* MBA guy. A flat as spacious as his in Bandra, thrice the size of my shithole in Malad—it probably cost him six times as much as mine. The door opened facing a kitchen and a bedroom, which was a bit awkward, but the glowing white of its walls, the sparkle of its creamy tiles and its generally minimalistic look made one forget those things. On the immediate right, there was a door to another room, which T promptly shut. I asked him if he shared the flat with someone. No, I like having two rooms, he said.

Past the entrance to the room which T had closed, there was the large living room, also on the right side. He took me there, and we sat on different sofas, both waiting for the first words to be uttered in this new janata-less zone. There was a table in one corner of the room, its round glass top naked and cracked. I was curious about the history of that crack; I couldn't imagine T causing it.

Actually, if T had said the right words then, I would have given myself to him. But he didn't look like he wanted to say anything, or he looked like he was deliberating, like he had all the time in the world. Wasn't it he who had suggested we get out of Janata?

Thinking of a way of moving forward, I said, Can I see your library?

T looked about for a few seconds. No, he said then. Because it's in the other room.

What the fuck, I thought, though I didn't bother asking him further. I had believed that he had stacks of books in a cupboard or in a rack. He didn't. Perhaps he only had a couple of books that he borrowed or stole from friends. Perhaps T was not the reader I thought he was. Or maybe he did have a library inside that room, and maybe he had a neurotic reason for barring entry. Maybe there was someone in that room right now, some drugged girl that he had met just before me and raped multiple times. Or maybe there was a corpse that he had forgotten about and remembered just in time, a corpse twisted in a way only death can achieve. Maybe the room was strewn with syringes that he had been using to serve his addictions, or maybe there were ghosts there, soporific ghosts who would awaken if they sensed a foreign presence. My thoughts were morbid but, perversely, I liked thinking them. They made me feel I was still myself, even after so much whiskey.

I'm paranoid at times. I've learnt to live with it.

T opened a bottle of expensive whiskey. We must have talked about something then, but I don't remember what. The air conditioner was running at just the right temperature. Good whiskey flowed. I began to relax a bit.

Perhaps we passed an hour like this, perhaps two, though it was sure that we were getting drunker by the minute. And then T called for my attention, he asked me, without warning, without context, if I would like to have him read a chapter of his novel.

No doubt I would, I slurred. It is still a novel in progress, he gave me the disclaimer. I don't care, I said. I didn't.

T went inside the other room and emerged with a sheaf of papers. He placed himself on the same wide sofa I was seated on. The distance between us was less than two feet.

He started reading. The chapter was about a man, quite like him, taking a train from Bandra to Churchgate to work. Stations passed, and the third-person narrator spoke of the many quotidian details of taking a morning train—the rush, the smell of sweat, the noise, the newspapers, the students, the beggars, the hijras. It was boring to begin with, but I allowed T to read on. As the young man alighted at Churchgate, the narrator came up with a metaphor, a metaphor that had something to do with leaving a manageable system (the train compartment) and entering the larger chaos of the world (the station) every day. It was a metaphor that I wasn't sure I grasped the total significance of. The man reached his office and logged in to his computer, and felt, for the nth time, how boring and meaningless every workday was—nicotine, caffeine, furtive reading-and-writing as ways to pass his ten hours at work. The initial boredom of T's text slowly mutated into a kind of unease, even horror. I thought this was symptomatic of my drunken state, but then I understood it as an organic effect created by the text itself, though I couldn't pinpoint how. T read on as a fear began to settle in my heart and I moved closer to him, almost touching him. The man left the office and walked through the traffic to go to a nearby restaurant to have dinner, the same food in the same restaurant, every day. He went to a bookstore after dinner and walked through the large racks where silly bestsellers stood menacingly. He then walked to Churchgate station to take the train back to Bandra, where he dithered about taking the train—as if there were something else that he could do at the station. T read on as the man watched the train start and move away from him and pick up speed. The man then began to run after the train, finally jumped to get inside or to enable an accident, like a foot slipping on the edge of the compartment door, an accident that would only partly be his making. The man then sat in the near-empty compartment and perceived, in the dangling handles overhead, the absence of souls in this city. The stations passed again in the reverse order, and as a vague memory took hold of the young man, he took out a pen and a piece of paper from his pocket and wrote a poem—and then T read that poem and I clutched my heart, and I held T's shirt because the poem was the most beautiful poem I had come across in my life. It was a small poem and it was a beautiful poem, so very beautiful that T choked on its last words and all the whiskey drained out of my head. That was the end of the chapter, and I whispered to T to read the poem again, and this time he read it a little less intimately, a little less personally, and although I'd then memorized the words, I cannot recollect them today.

Of course there was silence after that, like the silence on the other side of a commotion. Perhaps it is my imagination now that tells me that T was shaking. Perhaps he really was. Could I hear his heartbeat? Very possible, for I was almost in his arms, cuddling with him out of trepidation or something else. Anything could have happened. Something *should* have happened. I wanted it to happen. More whiskey, T asked, pushing me slightly away. I said yes, and T fixed me another drink. I'm sleepy, I said. Finish this last drink and then you can sleep, he said. No, let's sleep.

He took me to the room that was not closed, switched on the air conditioner there and gave me a sheet to cover myself with. Sleep, he said. I was surprised. I was surprised he didn't have a clue regarding what should have been the natural course of such a night, and I realized this was the kind of man you had to hand-hold right till the brink. So I said, won't you sleep with me? It's okay, I'll sleep in the other room, he said.

I was disappointed, but I don't think it took me long to fall asleep. I had a dream in which I saw a room with towers of books and papers, and ghosts of writers billowing about in post-mortal confusion. I saw a man sleeping naked on the floor of this room—a man sleeping in a fetal position, with his thumb in his mouth. I sensed this man was T although I wanted to make sure; but my dream wouldn't allow me a close-up, and perhaps this uncertainty was for my own benefit for I did not really want to know if this man was T, for that surety would have then converted—somehow, I don't know how—this dream into a nightmare. Nevertheless the dream went on without a plot, like dreams do. It was a dream stuck in a room where nothing interesting happened, where the main character just slept. To tell the truth, it was a boring dream, a boring dream that recurred all night.

I woke up early, close to four. It was still dark outside and I was dehydrated. I went to the kitchen and opened the fridge to drink some water. There was nothing in T's fridge except water and whiskey and wine. I opened the cabinets above the stove—there was nothing there either. I wondered if the house had always been like this, or if T was in the process of leaving it.

I decided I would go into T's room then, but as I pushed the door I found that it was locked from the inside. I felt a terrible loneliness—something related to the emptiness of T's apartment, perhaps. I left the place in the next five minutes.

I took an auto to Malad. The auto seemed to glide over the road, and I mused that my life was a like a road being swallowed by a vehicle moving ahead with insufficient headlights. The sky was womb-dark.

Over the next few days, I thought of T many times, and I sometimes thought of the secrets that he hid in the other room. I tried to make sense of what had really happened in our first meeting, or whether anything substantial had happened at all. Other than that, I met a rich friend who had recently turned into a communist: a believer in the possibility of a leftist social transformation, as he called it. Once, this guy drove me from work to his flat in Worli and showed me YouTube videos of a rabid leftist philosopher. He waited for me to be impressed, which I wasn't. We eventually ended up sleeping together and he turned out to be more than half-decent in bed.

During this time, I chatted online a couple of times with T, nothing more substantial than the usual hi and hello. I didn't know if we should meet again, or if it was I who should be the one asking for it. Then one Friday, T wrote to me: I'm alone. Do you mind meeting me?

The second meeting also took place in Janata Bar, two weeks after the first.

We ordered rum and cola. He looked good. He was not in formals that day, which meant that he had made the effort to go home after office and change for the occasion. He was in a loose polo and jeans, and looked handsome. I think I was wearing a grey tank top and blue jeans, or maybe I was wearing a salwaar-kameez. I don't exactly remember.

Soon our moods lightened and we shared the same jokes that we had cracked at our previous meeting, which according to me is a sign of deepening friendship. Once again, T never really laughed, just smiled.

When we finished a quarter of rum, he stopped me from ordering a repeat. He said, let me take you somewhere else today. Where? Somewhere close, to a friend's place. We can walk there.

We went to a building not very far from Janata Bar and very close to T's flat. We climbed the four floors we needed to and rang the bell to an apartment, whose heavy door could not quite hide the hilarity that came from behind it. The door was opened by a guy with bloodshot eyes who smiled a drooly, otiose smile—and who took great pains to introduce himself, but whose name I cannot now place conclusively between Sridhar and Sriram.

Inside the living room, there were ten or so people and half of them were girls. The flat was as spacious as T's. All the girls were prettier than me. In fact, all of them were almost grotesquely pretty, with lipstick and nail polish and rouged cheeks. It took me a while to adjust.

The room was inordinately hot for some reason, and it felt as if we were inside a warm beer bottle, tipsily coagulating. There was an air conditioner, but it wasn't functioning. The ceiling fan seemed to be complaining about the number of people it had to serve. There was a couch facing a TV that hung on the opposite wall, and two people sat on it playing a videogame while the rest talked or drank or strummed a guitar or passed a joint. T and I took a drag each, and T decided that the stuff was too strong. I liked him for doing that, for deciding for me.

The atmosphere in that living room was like a sluggish carnival, and just like in a carnival, it wasn't certain that everyone knew everyone else. T knew all the guys present, and sometimes they'd call each other by nicknames. The girls, however, were almost summarily unknown. Just who had invited them remained unclear. They had names like Preity and Sonu and Shazia which—compared to the guy's names like Sriram/Shridhar, Mohit, Ameya—seemed a bit insincere. No one knew me either, and with this thought I settled back into my chair and looked at the toil of the ceiling fan. Perhaps the drag hit me now, for I thought that all the women here were whores. Was I a whore? I looked at T, and he was smiling this wrinkle-producing smile of his, a smile that I only now realized I'd classified as *wrinkle-producing.*

Suddenly it was our turn to sit on the couch. T placed a controller in my hand and explained to me the maneuvers of the game we were to play. It was called FIFA and it was about simulation football. He told me what I would need to do to score. I told him that I'd never played a videogame in my life and that making me play would be a waste of time. At this, the other participants in the room, the men, got excited and told me that all of them had one fine day played the game for the first time and gradually became better at it and the same would be true for me too. The first thing to do was to choose a team to play with. A guy stepped in and gave us the idea that Spain, the football team Spain, was the strongest team in FIFA and that, because I was weak, I should play with Spain. Another guy came in and suggested that T should play with India, for India was a weak team, and India was India, and T was a good player. The game began. Some of the guys laughed, though

I didn't get the joke. I looked at the screen and the chaos on the screen—miniature electronic illusions flitting like flies—and I couldn't make out what was happening and what buttons I needed to press. I pressed all the buttons that I could at all times and I'm not sure if anything happened. T asked me to calm down. Every now and then he would say wow or shit and I wouldn't understand what it was supposed to mean. And then he scored against me. India went up 1:0 against Spain. Then he scored again, and then once more. Each time he scored, he would exult for a microsecond and then give that crow-feet smile of his, a smile that he thought he generated only for himself, though I was always noticing. The other guys would laugh and high-five; apparently everyone found India scoring against Spain comical, and I had mixed feelings about how they were reacting. Soon it was half-time, and players from my side looked to the turf and walked back into the dressing room dejectedly, their faces showing an electronic emotion they shared with me to a lesser degree. The computer commentator said something horrible about Spain's performance. A joint was being passed around and, unthinkingly, I took another drag. T looked at me but said nothing. Instead he poured himself a shot of whiskey from a nearby bottle and took a large gulp. The next half began, and for some reason, I resolved to play better. I narrowed my eyes and made sense of the colourful figures trotting about on the screen. I figured where the ball was. I pressed the buttons one by one and figured out what they did. T kept saying wow and shit intermittently. I played as if the reason for my existence were to keep the ball and pass it to someone who was Spain. The guys around us were not laughing as much now, or if they were, it was about something else and not the game. I passed the ball around and T's players kept chasing the ball, and this routine was almost turning banal when, all of a sudden, something extraordinary happened: one of my players closed in on the goal and actually put the ball into it. The net shook in an exaggerated fashion. I don't know what got into me just then, because I jumped from the couch and hopped up and down and kept shrieking—wow, wow, wow—while T looked at me and gave me a wrinkly smile and topped up another shot of the whiskey. Everyone around us looked at me with wide eyes. Although I settled back into the couch, my heart was still beating wildly as I thought I had achieved something big, something that would at once announce my arrival as a potent person into this milieu, or perhaps even into the world. But as soon as I thought about it again it made me sad—an incalculable sadness—and I was on the verge of tears, as if my whole life till then had been a random walk into nothingness, as if this was all there was left for me to achieve, a stupid outcome in a stupid videogame, and I put the controller down and pulled T to me and said, let's go.

We left the place hurriedly and walked toward T's apartment. While climbing the stairs, I asked him why he had taken me to his friend's place. He couldn't answer for a while, and his silence told me that he was thinking about the question, which meant that the question was somehow important to him, even though I don't think I meant it that way. He spoke while turning the key to his apartment. He said he took me there because he didn't want to bring me here.

Inside his apartment, the door to the other room was open, but before I could peer in, he shut it. We settled in the living room and he brought two glasses of wine. I asked him why he didn't want to bring me to his place. He said that if he had brought me to his place, which he had done now, he would have asked me if I had liked the chapter that he had read to me the last time.

I guess I was relieved. I told him that I'd loved that chapter. Didn't you see how speechless I was after it, I said. But that was it, I didn't say more, though I knew that there was something else to be said. There is always something more to say after someone shows you their writing. The $(n+1)^{th}$ comment has weight, I thought. But I remained silent. In fact, I was scared I would say something stupid. And although I could see some discomfort on his face, T didn't push me to talk any further. In that long silence, during which I tried to act as if the glass I was sipping from was not the first glass of wine I had ever had, I also decided that I will fuck him that night no matter what.

I've never seen anyone score in their first game, he said. Maybe that was because you were playing with Spain and I was playing with India.

Maybe, I said.

Do you want me to read you another chapter, T asked.

I would love for you to, but tonight I've something else on my mind, I said.

What?

Your novel is going to be great, I said.

Really?

Yes, it is going to be great, I said. And we will have enough time to read all your chapters.

So what is on your mind tonight, he asked.

Fucking you, I said.

Hearing this, T coughed loudly and disbelievingly. He coughed so much that I thought the wine from his glass would spill and make a bloody wound on the tiles. He coughed and coughed, as if he were being choked to death. And it was somewhere during this coughing that we ended up coming close to each other. Then, when his coughing subsided, we kissed. We fondled each other, pressed into each other. He lifted me up and took me to the bedroom, the bedroom right in front of the entrance, the bedroom that was not the other room. We were going to begin at last, I thought.

Then suddenly I remembered. I might be bleeding a bit, I gave the disclaimer.

What do you mean, he asked.

I mean I had the last day of my period yesterday, I said.

I don't care, he said.

Yeah?

Yes, I'm sure, Europeans do it during their periods, he said.

I found it weird that he would justify it like that. What did Europeans have to do with it? It changed something in me, something crucial. It was as if we had teleported to another planet, a planet in which I was closer to my real wants.

What is in the other room? I asked.

What?

What is in the other room? I repeated.

Why do you ask me this? he asked.

I want us to do it in the other room.

Why?

I knew I had put the moment in jeopardy. But I couldn't stop. I want to do it in the other room, I said.

But why? Why do you insist on going to that room?

I don't know, I said, why are you so secretive about it?

I'm not secretive about it, it's just privacy, he replied.

And is what we are going to do a public thing, I asked.

Pfft, he exhaled.

Pfft, I exhaled in mimicry.

I don't understand, he said.

I don't understand either, I said. What do you have in that room? A graveyard?

He didn't answer. I tried to kiss him again. He let me, but it was not like before. Please, I said. I still didn't know why I was insistent.

Please, he answered, circumflexing his eyebrows.

We stopped. We stopped and there was an eternity between us. Or a truth hung in an aleatory setup. An unsurpassable truth, unknowable and invisible, but very present. I realized that it was the planet of this truth that I had taken us to. I straightened my clothes, hating myself. T didn't move an inch. He was looking down at the floor, staring into a void that had nothing to do with the floor. Was there a tear in his eye? I couldn't say. I gathered my belongings and made to leave. I stumbled on something. I was too drunk.

You can sleep here, T said.

NO, I shouted, and then I lost my footing and fell.

I don't know what happened or did not happen immediately after that. When I woke up, I found myself on the bed alone, a sheet draped over me. Some hours had passed; perhaps it was again four in the morning. Eternal fucking recurrence, I thought.

I was dehydrated and went to the kitchen and drank some water, and then I pushed the door to the other room. It was not locked! I went inside. T was sleeping on a large bed, opposite which was a huge shelf with books. Classic fiction, contemporary literary fiction, some poetry. Big fat dictionaries. English, Hindi, French. A lot of stuff in Hindi. Beside the shelf, there was a large wall-hanging with grooves for photos. Dozens of photos. Photos of a beautiful woman, a white woman, photos of T with this woman, this woman who was definitely his lover. T and this woman on the top of a mountain,

T and this woman in a desert, T and this woman beside pine trees, T and this woman on a bed, almost naked ...

I looked around. It looked like a room that had been set by a woman and upset by a man. I opened the two cupboards. One had T's crumpled clothes, all a sorry mess. The other cupboard was clean and empty. I sensed that it had been recently vacated. I thought of the word *European*. I thought of the word *graveyard*. His woman had left him. Just then I heard a rustle from behind me. I turned. It was T, awake, sitting on his bed with his knees in his hands. I tried to mumble something. He lunged at me from the bed, and I shrieked. He held my head in his hands, pressing my cheeks with the heel of his palms, as if to kiss me. I struggled out of his grip, my fear giving me strength. I rushed out of the room, went to the other one to pick up my stuff, and left the house. I climbed down the stairs, looking up frantically to see if T had followed me. On the street, it took me a long ten minutes to find an auto. Once inside, I felt the road being swallowed once again by the auto. I sighed, looked. This time there was a break of light in the sky, this time there were grey clouds in the sky, and this time everything was not black but grey. I thought that the auto was going straight to heaven, that I was dead and the auto was going straight to heaven, and then, emerging from a strange place that had somehow been accessed, a poem formed in me and I memorized it, and when I reached home I wrote the poem down on my computer. I realized that this would be a poem so dear to me that I would never show it to anyone else. Then I broke all that could connect me to T online, forever. For the next few minutes I read my poem to myself, again and again, till I fell asleep. In that light sleep I dreamt of a FIFA match, of two electronic teams playing against each other. But one of the teams was stationary. Perhaps this team was not interested, or perhaps it was only a collection of shadows. The other team was performing all its movements again and again. It was difficult to say if I was controlling things; and it was difficult to say if there was any winning or losing.

~~~~

Hi S,

It is tough to be objective about this story, but I'm really interested to know the poem you mention at the end, which, I believe, is the kind of readerly curiosity that should register as writerly success. I think you've done well here.

I did change my house. Thanks for asking; I appreciate your concern.

About traveling: well, she has asked me to spend some time with her in Interlaken. As a friend. I'd be lying if I said I'm not thinking about it.
~~~~

I'm taking the liberty of sending you a couple of my own pieces. Maybe we can continue talking this way, sharing our writing with each other, updating each other with the mess of our fictions and realities, our memories and fantasies. That is the mess that we are, right?

I think 'The Other Room' is a good title for your story.

Best,

T

P.S. Her name is Anne-Marie, and I loved her in a way that Love isn't used to anymore. That night I'd been dreaming about her, and when I woke up I thought you were her. Of what happened, that is the bit I'm sure of.

P.P.S. The girls in Sriram's apartment were not call girls. They were from his neighbouring flat.

~~~~
~~~~

Flashback to a Sunday Morning

They who love each other live in a two-bedroom flat in Pali Naka, Bandra, paying considerable rent. She is French and he is Indian.

Like every other piece of furniture in their second-floor flat, the table in the living room belongs to the landlord. Its circular glass top is four feet in diameter. The centre of this top is placed on a thick wooden cylinder which goes down and splits into three baroque legs that touch the floor like closed fists. The tabletop is covered with a circular tablecloth, which is whitened here and there with a faint haze of flour; a few purple spots can also be seen on it. This is all spillage from breakfast.

For breakfast they ate:

- Two out of the four pomegranates they purchased last evening from Pali Naka market and which were peeled shoddily by him in the morning with the help of a short blunt made-in-Italy knife. The seeds of one fruit were redder than the other, and he let her have most of these.

The burst and squeeze of these seeds is the source of the purple spots.

- Three slices each of the rye bread she purchased last weekend from Le Pain Quotidien, a French chain that has recently opened a bakery in Colaba, and which she froze immediately after coming home. The crust of the bread comes covered with white flour which sheds itself on the tablecloth whenever they eat slices of it.
- Some homemade butter from milk bought every day from a nearby milk vendor, who has been running this business for a long time in Bandra and charges a hefty premium for purity. She is not very good at keeping watch over boiling milk though, and has spilt it many times. They never fight about spilt milk.
- Conserves—apricot, papaya-ginger and gooseberry—which they bought from FabIndia at Pali Hill two weeks back. This morning, he used a different spread on each slice, while she stuck to the gooseberry. On the tablecloth there is a little smudge of orange, most likely an errant from the gooseberry conserve.

They have no use for the extra bedroom; they have never slept there or made love there in the two years they have been in this flat. Her father used the room when he visited them a couple of months ago. He had come from Vannes in Brittany, her hometown, and although he had expressed concern regarding the loud honking on the streets of Bandra, he was seemingly content with their apartment and its comforts. The previous summer, they had let the extra bedroom to an acquaintance, a senior from their business school (their love story had started in a well-known institute of management in western India), for three months. The man, working in the same consulting company as her, but at a higher position involving more business travel, hardly ever stayed in the flat, but paid his half of the rent in cash. This made them happy. But this man never paid the electricity bill despite having used the air conditioner for the entire duration of his short stays in the flat. This made them unhappy, though not in equal measure. He didn't want to ask the man for the electricity money because it wasn't much. She wanted the man to pay. In the end, she managed to make the man pay.

They are seated at the table opposite each other. She is wearing an all-black Nike running gear, without the shoes though, and looking intently into the screen of her large Lenovo laptop. She is wearing sports gear because everything else she usually dons at home is currently inside the washing machine. The machine, tucked in a little corner of the kitchen, is creating a sinusoidal hum that reaches them intermittently, at each of its crests, mixed with a little shudder that is created when the oscillating body strikes against the wall behind it.

Her top has an inch-wide strap at each shoulder. The straps cross each other on the back and meet the rest of the fabric just below the shoulder blades. This arrangement heightens the perception of muscularity, something that he is aware of even though he has not seen her from behind today. He has always found this top incredibly sexy on her. And this is part of the reason why she has chosen to wear it now instead of one of his loose t-shirts.

She is working on the eighty-seventh slide of a presentation which will be used in a strategy workshop for a client in Delhi. She has to travel to Delhi tomorrow morning for the workshop. The client, a gigantic energy company, is looking for focus in their renewable energy segment. Acquiring smaller, more agile companies is not ruled out and will most likely be the major recommendation. The exact question on her mind currently is the font-size for a text box which includes the three salient features of one such potential acquisition target.

He knows and likes the intensity with which she does her work. He likes her attention to detail, her ill-disposition toward procrastination, her sense of possibility.

Her lips are pouted in concentration. Her blond hair is slightly rumpled on the left side because she has a habit of itching there when she is thinking. Some strands of her hair have risen to form distinct, fragile arches. One side of her face is glowing in the morning sunlight that enters the room from the large sliding window on her left. Just below the window is the power socket to which a corded plug from her laptop is attached. The laptop has a faulty battery; it needs to be powered all the time. It irritates her a lot.

He likes this mild irritation too.

He is sitting exactly opposite her, closer to the wall that separates the living room and their bedroom, with his back to it. In front of him, on the table, lie a large dictionary and several sheets of paper strewn in disorder. The front jacket of the dictionary says: *Harrap's Shorter English to French || French to English Dictionary*. He finds the 'shorter' in the title funny because the dictionary is massive; it is difficult for him to hold in one hand.

Most of the pieces of paper are printouts he took from his office yesterday. He works in an insurance company, in an ambiguous role that is neither in sales nor in operations, and so it allows him many free hours. He can be unmindful of details, procrastinate; he is in the habit of using the office printer a lot—for printing short stories, poems, articles. Sometimes she scolds him lovingly for wasting so much paper.

Some of the pages he printed yesterday have tables with two columns. The left column has French text:

Nous étions à l'Étude, quand le Proviseur entra, suivi d'un nouveau habillé en bourgeois et d'un garçon de classe qui portait un grand pupitre.

And the right column has its translation in English:

We were in class when the headmaster entered, followed by a new fellow dressed in common clothes and a school servant carrying a large desk.

On the blank side of some printouts are his handwritten notes, a sample of which reads thus:

étions = IMPERFECT {être = to be}

j' étais

tu étais

il était

nous étions

vous étiez

ils étaient

As is obvious, he is learning French. But his is a top-to-bottom approach to the language. Four days ago, on an impulse, he copied the French and English versions of the first chapter of *Madame Bovary* from gutenberg.org and placed them side by side in a word document. Thereafter, he classified all newly encountered words into nouns, verbs, adjectives, adverbs and common phrases, classified them to the best of his ability and put them in another document. After reading each paragraph twice in French and then gathering its meaning from the English text, he is now trying to absorb each word of the original—to remember its meaning—by building a memory of its usage in *Madame Bovary*, using either the word's dictionary listing or, in case of verbs, the information from the grammar section of the dictionary. Verbs are aplenty and also the most cumbersome to get at because their forms keep changing. He works a bit differently with them, first identifying the tense in which he encounters them and then listing down all the variations within that tense. He thinks that he has made good progress with verbs. Out of repetition, the first part—tense identification—has now become almost automatic. He can also guess, with almost ninety per cent accuracy now, all the various forms of the verb in the identified tense.

In the last four days, his persistence with this method of learning French has given birth to a quixotic sense of possibility in him, that of being able to read large novels in French all by himself. His aim is to finish *Madame Bovary* first. He believes that once he has trudged through the first hundred or so pages in this assiduous fashion, he will not have to depend on the dictionary at all. He will be able to scorch through the rest of the text then, he thinks, with a mastery of the imperfect and the past historic tenses. But somewhere within his mind, the possibility of losing interest midway and thus abandoning the project—like other similar projects of his life—has taken root. He also knows that this is how he is, a person who takes on a Herculean task with an indelible faith in his own doggedness, eventually ending up with mixed results.

What gives him joy is playing with the new language. He has jumbled some of the new words he has learnt into new phrases and sentences. Often his phrases seek rhyme at the cost of meaning. At other times he just follows the permutations that his heart provides readily. What comes out in any case is interesting, and the rhyming serves him as a tool to remember the trickiness of French pronunciation; it reminds him how he cannot read French like English.

Some of his creations, his jumbled rhymes and phrases, are typed on the back of one of the papers. Below each of these lines are written, in English, their meanings. These are written in a handwriting different from his. Compared to his sharp-edged letters inside the parentheses, this handwriting has shorter, rounder forms, with a lot of space given to the twirls of the l's and the circles of the r's, but with hurried m's and n's which merge with the next letter almost a bit too soon. This is her handwriting.

d'un coup de coude, et le casquette de loutre, tomba tomba tomba! (adaptation of a line from *Madame Bovary*)

a nudge, and the otter cap, fell fell fell!

Cependant c'est pendant … (the pronunciation of the first word and the next two together is the same)

However it was during …

Le ciel parle en demi-voix, pendant la nuit, garnis par douleur. (invented, just like that)

The sky talks in whispers during the night, garnished with sadness.

Paris, sans la Seine, à peine, existe. (invented, just like that; I suppose it rhymes in the middle)

Paris without the Seine hardly exists.

peur par le toupet de cochon … (random combination, ha ha ha)

frightened by the cheek of pigs …

She first saw these creations last night when he gave the sheet to her and asked her to note the meanings. But precisely because she was closer to the meanings than he could be, she couldn't help but marvel at his inventiveness. She found the last construction funny. 'It is something that,' she said, 'no one French can ever come up with, for it is so absurd to be scared of the bravery of pigs. And why pigs, suddenly, out of the blue?' He told her that all the words were from the first chapter of *Madame Bovary*. At this, she remarked that his was an extraordinary attempt. The one about Paris and Seine was the most poetic, according to her. She then called him *un garçon mignon* and other sweet nothings. The added tenderness in bed last night can be attributed to his novel attempts at playing with French.

Currently he is wearing a yellow t-shirt, a bit faded from repeated washes. She had gifted this shirt to him when they had visited Bali together, about nine months ago. Next month, they are going on another vacation, to trek at high altitudes in Nepal.

Proud of the tinge of mental fatigue he now feels, he tenderly moves his palm over the many papers in front of him, thinking of just how much he loves her, how his learning French is his way to belong even more to her. In her dreams she sometimes babbles in French, and he knows he wants to understand what she says. But can he really learn French like this? This question exists, but does not sting at this moment. It seems a mellow question. Or a question flooded in some benign waters. Somewhere in the back of his mind, an amorphous swamp has taken over. Or not a swamp but an idyll. This idyll may be the space of a feeling, or a realization, or the kind of epiphany that one experiences in the most banal of moments, moments in which nothing extraordinary happens, moments which can be called 'coagulated,' moments which are loaded with the present, moments referring to beautiful histories, pointing to futures perfectly devoid of destinations. The idyll in his head, its smooth inebriation, is a product of living through the happiest moment of his life.

Just now, on this Sunday no different from other Sundays.

But behind the idyll, behind the apparent beauty, there lurks something grey. He wants to be a writer. He wants to be a writer, he has known that for some time, but he often finds himself with nothing to say. Every second of his leisure that he spends learning French is a second he is not writing. His biggest fear is that he may have no story to tell. But he also knows that the only way to find one is to keep at it, the writing. His ambition for writing is the grey element of all his moments.

Moreover, the knowledge that he has just lived the happiest moment of his life brings with it the idea of the imminent loss of that moment, the idea that no other moment will ever surpass it.

Maybe when they have their first child he will reach a level of happiness that he cannot even conceive of right now. He spends a whole minute thinking of making a child with her, a possibility that they have discussed many times. Then he rises from his seat, goes up to her. She is startled, but then they kiss passionately.

Flashback to Nepal Holiday

It is the fourth hour of the journey now, and we have just entered the mountains. She has the window seat, but our heads are pressed together as both of us look outside. There is green and golden paddy on distant hilly terraces. A white passenger two seats ahead, excited by the sudden picturesqueness of the view, takes many pictures.

I think the picturesque has only a stale, postcard beauty. A contemporary artist is probably not interested in the entire valley anymore, but in bits of the valley, bits that are indecipherable and could be from anywhere. I imagine zooming into that system of paddy terraces. Zooming in, not going close, so that the details are fudged. Zooming in enough and then framing three to four levels of paddy. Three to four terraces, that is. And then click. What? Blurry goldenrod. A work of art.

The mountain path is uneven, dusty. The bus struggles through it, sometimes tilting so much as to make us tense in the opposite direction. I place her hand over my thigh and caress her fingers. Some of the passengers cough from the dust whirled up by the grinding tyres. The dust is fine and powdery, the kind that sticks to the throat.

The bus finally stops for a break. The passengers get down and clear their nasal passages and spit. *Aakhthoo*. Like in Hindi literature. Always the Aakh- before the -thoo.

We see two European girls titter at this carnival of spitting. She, my love, Anne-Marie, also spits. Without the Aakh-. Her spit falls on the dusty road and becomes beady. For some reason I frame that image in my mind.

After the break, the bus starts its gritty maneuvering again. Soon members of the six-seven-eight-thousand-metres club appear suspended in the sky. She grows excited, points at them. Then they hide behind the groves of pine on the nearer mountains.

There is an obscure song playing for the umpteenth time in the bus. A woman on the seat in front of us is about to puke. A sleepy man on a seat to our left bangs his head on the seat in front of him. Someone farts hideously. After some zigzagging, the snowy peaks reappear. 'The nearer you go, the taller they become,' she says. 'They become impossible, no?'

'That's trigonometry,' I point out.

The town where the bus eventually drops us, and from where the walking will begin tomorrow, is a one-road town, like in Western movies. The town is like a Mexican town. The town is like a Peruvian town. I don't know. The town has many places to eat and drink and none of these places have more than four tables, and all of them serve momos. The town has many sparkling children. The town has many snotty stars. Looking up from the middle of the road, I can see the Milky Way cloud the black sky. 'Not many towns look up like that,' she says. The town is ugly. The town is so foreign, so beat-down, so melancholy, it terrorizes me to imagine the lives of the townspeople. The town is a one-night town. The town has street dogs. The town doesn't have streetlights. Apart from the crickets and the dogs and the loud river running parallel to it, the town is quiet. The town sleeps early. Now and then the dogs cry.

Our first walk the next morning is on a trail littered with mule shit and the footprints of trekkers before us. The river gushes a hundred or so feet below on the right, flowing opposite to the direction of our advance.

In the beginning there were villages and fields. Paddy, sugarcane, soybean. Colonies of radish. A soybean pod is like a pea pod, in case you didn't know.

At times a system of golden paddy terraces ends at one side of the trail and then continues on the other side. Up close with the paddy, touching distance, she says, 'This is going to be beautiful.' And I wonder: How does experience become literature?

She pauses and takes pictures of the path, of the river, of the vegetation around us. She asks me to take pictures too. Sometimes we ask our guide to take pictures of us together. The pictures, whether clicked thoughtlessly by the guide or with much artifice by her and me, turn out fine.

Yesterday I thought I could zoom in on three to four levels of paddy and frame so as to make a work of—what?—abstract art? Today, inside the valley, having it unfold before me with the pace of one step following the other; today, with our pictures of the valley, with our story in it, that thought seems stale.

I am, or my gaze is, at the site of a bomb explosion. I see a hanging man. He is blown. All burnt flesh and scraps of cloth. Then I see a man standing to my right. He is the hanging man come to life. This man standing next to me is almost naked, save the smoking rags holding his body. The shirt used to have checks, I can make that out. Then to my left there appears an asphalt road on which there is a man on all fours. This man is different, a new character. The lower half of his body, facing me, is naked and scalding red, so red that it makes me shiver in my dream. Like confetti ribbons, bits of his shirt hang on the upper half of his body, but this time I cannot make out what pattern it used to have. I presume he is dead, somehow transfixed in that position by the explosion. But then he starts moving! His leg moves, then his arm. I'm stunned. He is moving in super slow motion. Each movement of his tightens my throat. I'm confused. Where is he trying to go? I want to know by looking in the direction of his movement, but the frame of my dream refuses to shift. He moves again. I'm terrified now. Not by the sight of him, but by his movement. Why is he moving? Where does he want to go? I want to know. I want to know.

I wake up. It is two or three in the morning, I reckon. I realize I need to take a piss. It is dark in the single-ply room we are holed up in. I can hear her calm breathing. I tiptoe, go outside. The sound of the river shakes me a bit. Sound-wise, a river is steady and infinite, a sea periodic. There is grey light all around, moonlight and starlight. Still dazed by my dream, I smash the big toe of my left foot on a stone and it hurts stupendously. I take my piss. When I return to the room I'm thinking of my toe and my dream. I should disinfect the toe, but I'm too lazy to locate the med box in the room's darkness. My toe throbs. I'm worried about it. Maybe it will give me gangrene? I try to remember the dream again, to be able to write about it. I close my eyes and reconstruct it. The river goes on like a fire. Then I sleep.

The toe isn't too badly hurt. She bandages it in the morning, after berating me for not waking her up in the night.

We walk alongside the river, on and on, sometimes to this side sometimes to that, crisscrossing on bridges, always against the flow of water, like scientists intent on discovering the root of a thing. As I walk on in slight pain, I try to understand my dream by wrapping it in words and making a sentence out of it. *Hot destruction, dreamt from a cold, dark, peaceful room.* Once I make this sentence, I deliberate on the process of making this sentence. The desire to be a writer is probably the desire to compress reality into sentences. Or vice versa.

And at the day's end I write some sentences in a diary:

1. Mules panniered and packsaddled pelt the stony path with pensive eyes, but be careful and lean on the mountain when giving way, for these mules here are innocent enough to unknowingly nudge you into a hundred-metres gorge down which you will rumble and tumble till your unhinged insensate body meets the marching river and the number of fractures in your skull alone exceed the number of god-given bones you had in your unbroken version.
2. Flowerless magnolia, flowerless rhododendron, this is not the season for flowers.
3. Barren bistre bluffs. Military-green hills. Mountains girting a cloud forest. Mountains leaking filamentous waterfalls. Mountains separated by a river. Mountains separated by a river and joined by a pendulous bridge. Ecru cliffs running beside the river with black tops as if a huge box of black paint were spilt carelessly over them. Mountains populated with straight dark-green pines that grow only till a certain altitude. Lichen-mottled mountains. Dark chocolate mountains. Pewter mountains suggesting the excess of some mineral. Black mountains. Black mountains scratched by a celestial claw revealing their white frozen scab. Snow-draped mountains that would make excellent ski stations if only you could

reach them. Mountains like a many-edged object wrapped tautly in a terrific white sheet. Incandescent mountains. Mountains nudged by cirri. Cone heads, buttes and mesas. Mountains with eskers tracing avalanches ancient and recent. Nacreous glaciered mountains neutered of life. Mountains reflected in lakes. Mountains that bequeath stillness and resolution, and educate of the concept of littleness. Youngest mountains in the world.

4. For writers, writing is dreaming. For dreamers, dreaming is writing.
5. The slow pace of writing—slower than pure telling—forces upon the act of remembering the dream an excess, an over-remembering, that facilitates the constructive process of filling-in of the holes in that slowly-evoked memory.

During our walk the next day, I find myself constructing sentences from what I observe, and also stressing to remember them for the evening scribble. I feel that I have found a *way*: If I can record experience in sentences and reproduce those sentences after a lag, there will be an aesthetic addition to reality. I might produce something akin to literature.

We pass through some sun-drenched villages, each with a dozen or so hovels shingled with a black stone that I would like to name exactly. The men are away working in the fields or elsewhere. The women are inside the houses, cooking or weaving or idling. The narrow streets of the entire village are left for children to concoct games. As we pass, some children form a group and gape at us. They all wail *namaste* in a failed chorus. The youngest of them is no more than eighteen months old and he fails a bit in performing his namaste, one palm going higher than the other. The other children follow with their raucous salutations which we have grown tired of hearing: 'Give me pen, give me balloon. Give me pen, give me balloon …'

We eat a local dish called dhindo for lunch in the dung-strewn front yard of a village house, and from there we can see an eight-thousand-metres-high mountain, standing calm and patient and majestic, steaming a little cloud in the strong sun. Earlier, as we walked, this giant would sometimes hide behind a nearer mountain, with only the tiniest triangle of its summit showing like a bleached white monastery hiding a god. In this village there is also a real monastery surrounded by kerfs of black stone I would like to name the type of. Between the ragged triangles of those stones, the monastery compound looks like the epicentre of an earthquake. In the front yard of the house we are in, two belled and furred calves of a milk-giving animal I would like to name exactly (likely a cross between a cow and a yak) chew on dried stalk amidst their own knotty, fragrant dung. As I look up to the white mountain, I notice that my view is being obstructed by four parallel telephone lines and two strings with a pattern of Tibetan flags—green orange white yellow blue. Aware of the obstructions now, I see only them and not the mountain. I wish for the fluttering flags to be and for the solid telephone lines to disappear. But then I discover that one end of both the flag-bearing strings is tied to the pole that supports the telephone lines. I notice in this a symbol for something but I can't make out what. The strings and the poles have learnt to live with each other, I tell myself, and I should learn to look at the mountain through them both. Then I look down and see the two calves gaping at me, and I notice how they are still and yet breathe so fast. Sometimes they twitch a nostril to shake off a fly.

We move on after lunch.

Things she said:

'It is good to walk in the sun, no?'

'It is good to walk in the shade, no?'

'It's beautiful, the forest, huh?'

'We walk more in the morning. I think we also walk faster in the morning. It is good to walk in the morning, no?'

'The first fifteen minutes in the morning are tough.'

'You should not let your cardio come down. You should slow down and find your pace. But you should not stop. When you stop, your cardio comes down. It is difficult to start again after your cardio is down.'

'I think we should take it easy today.'

'I have to wash. My feet are dirtier than yours. Because my shoes are more open than yours.'

'The vegetation is very recharging.'

'You walk faster when you walk in the front.'

'You are making a lot of dust walking in the front. I've to take all the dust.'

'Having a light in the room makes all the difference, no?'

'Fuck, there are mice in the room!'

'The mouse bit my sock. *Merde!*'

'And yours too. *Putain!*'

'*Dégueulasse.*'

'The view is beautiful, no?'

'The people are so mean, they're so money-minded, they think they have the right to loot tourists.'

'What does that mountain look like to you? To me it looks like an owl, with its two peaks like ears.'

'Crows in Mumbai do caw-caw. The crows here do aw-aw, no?'

'Your writing is so …'

'The camera batteries are dead. We should have got extra batteries.'

At our resting place for the day, I read bits of a novel. It begins as the protagonist, a man in his sixties, hears a strange rumble emanating from a distant mountain that is visible from his backyard. He associates the sound with that of approaching death. This beginning, its symbolic weight, makes me pause and listen to the high mountains in front of me. The nearest ones rise a kilometre above my eye level. As I look, the tops of the snowy mountains turn orange, then pink, then blue in the setting sun, but all there is to hear is the patchwork of inchoate sentences in my mind.

I read on. I read on as the old man has conversations with various members of his family, as he senses a personal failure in the impending failure of his children's marriages and so on … and everything in the novel is beautiful and flawed and subtle to the point of being hidden, and I look at the sky become lavender and swallow the remaining whiteness in the west, just above the highest mountain, and I read on and I suddenly think of the equanimity of this moment and the idea of my work life in Mumbai, sprawled in my mind like a monolith—neither the surface nor the depths of which I understand—and I worry over what to do with my writing, and my writing seems to me like a hard heavy brick made out of the glumly glued pages of many an interesting book, and I feel like pulling out my hair, and I feel that total lack of faith in all the sentences I have written and all the sentences I will write, and I grow convinced that I am not a writer but only a pretender, and my heart sinks in the way hearts have always sunk in life and in literature. And I read on, as the old man goes to his son's mistress and requests her to abort his bastard grandchild …and my love, Anne-Marie, comes up and hugs me from behind and says it's too cold outside, and I agree, and we look up at the sky and see Orion and we call it *The Roman Soldier* for the hundredth time, and we say *I love you* to each other for the millionth time, and I think I love her so much, as much as the Himalayas, but my heart is grey now and I am in her arms and I cannot read on.

PART TWO

The Bachelor

Losing Face

I am in the boss's cabin listening to him, and suddenly I feel my face flee. It is as if it is drifting sideways, toward the wall, or toward the translucent board that is riveted to the wall for scribbling thoughts. What do I do? I pucker and grimace, if these things are even possible now, to hold my face in its right place. My boss looks at me as if his own face has tightened in response to the spectacle of someone losing a face. Unfortunately I can't verify the feeling, because there are no mirrors in my boss's cabin, which is only proper—the absence of mirrors is a necessity to delete erotic possibilities from the workplace. So I ignore my fleeing face and try to concentrate on the words that my boss is uttering. There is something about lead and lag measures. If you do the lead measures right, then the lag measures, which is to say the results, will follow automatically. He wants me to make a model to track the correlation between the lead and the lag measures. The whole thing is too obvious to reveal any insight, I think. But I don't mention this, simply because my face is fleeing, or perhaps also because I've the notion that I'm wrong to think whatever I'm thinking, or perhaps I'm sure I'm thinking wrongly. I say nothing when the boss ends, not even *Absolutely* or *Sure* or *Will be done* or *Understood*, nothing in the vein of a parting remark whose sole purpose would have been to provide an artificial confidence to the boss. I know that both the remark that is expected of me and the confidence that is expected of the boss are important but empty gestures. I've nothing against empty gestures. It's just that I feel I've lost my face, which is quite a thing if you think about it.

So I just walk out of the cabin, longing for my palms to investigate my lost face. I reach my cubicle. I enter two sets of usernames and passwords into my laptop to reach the main screen. This entering of usernames and passwords is a reflex; I do it even when I've nothing to do on the computer. I stare at my screen—no files open, no files to open. Then suddenly I remember the story of my face. I poke with my fingers, then use my palms. The thing is there. It has returned!

There is No Home

The flat in Bandra became too big and too lonesome after she left me. The friends nearby were no help, lost as they were in their ganja and videogames. Now

I have a bachelor pad in Goregaon, which is where I am right now. And right now I am naked below my waist, carrying a Manto book in one hand and a glass of orange juice in another. It is morning. There is nothing much in my fridge apart from the orange juice, and like all mornings over the past few months, I will not be having breakfast today as well. I woke up half an hour back, and now I'm waiting for the geyser to heat up the water. Some minutes ago, I masturbated thinking of her, my love, on top of me and whispering into my ear, 'I like it when you hold my butt … hold my butt.' Then I texted her.

Last night I went to a seedy place called Shanghai Bar and had two big bottles of Kingfisher beer. That was dinner and lunch combined. On the little TV in the AC section, they had put on a channel that played old Hindi songs. I gaped at the TV and let myself feel lonely and schmaltzy. I thought of texting a girl I've come to know and whom I believe would be easy to sleep with, but I decided against it. Just as I paid my bill I felt a fear suck at my chest and I thought, there is no home. Then I went home.

I'm twenty-seven years old and I feel I'm at an edge.

In two hours I'll be back in the office again, as if returning to waking life after a litany of lethargic dreams. Last night I slept in two phases. In the first phase my mind kept flitting between memories and dreams, and all of them, in some way or the other, were fragments of the books I've read and the books I'm reading. Literature took my sleep away, I can say, and I claim that I even heard its gears shift in my head. The light was on, and at times in my half-sleep, tormented by images whose genesis lay in words, I would think that all I needed to go to real sleep was to switch the light off. But I was too lazy, or sleepy, to do that. Then, a couple of hours later, the scene-switching stopped, and the void of deep sleep, a void made possible by the exhaustion of literature's possibilities, presented itself with all its black beauty. I plunged into it and then emerged at 6:45 a.m., and the first thing I thought of was sex.

Social Life

I'm in my office again. I've just logged in. In half an hour, M, a girl from HR, will ask me to come to the canteen with her for breakfast. I don't want to go with her, but I never say no. M is only interested in building sexual tension. She talks to me about sex, says things like—*Size matters*, or *There are some guys who can't get it up without a BJ*, or *You shouldn't smoke so much, it will hamper your performance in bed.* She irritates me with all this innuendo, the sole function of which is to test how I face it. But

I never let anything show. I've even invited M to my new flat in Goregaon, twice, an act that to me denotes that my life is generally moving toward some catastrophe. But I made sure that M never came to my house alone. She came with one other woman on both occasions, either from the office or outside. We drink a bottle of horrible wine and mostly talk about relationships.

These three—M and her two friends—are the only people who have visited my flat. They call it a steal, considering the rent I pay. I could call it a steal too, considering the rent I used to pay in Bandra, when I was living with her, my love.

Introduction to 'The Bachelor'

After the breakfast with M, I get back to my desk and start reading. In the office I'm currently on to a pirated PDF of *Bartleby and Co.* by the Spanish writer Enrique Vila-Matas. The details of how I got this book on my office laptop are noteworthy. The insurance company I work in is very strict about IT security, but it somehow allows this one website that I use to download pirated e-books. That is how I got my reading material.

Bartleby and Co. is about the Bartleby Syndrome, which has to do with writers who don't write for one reason or another, basically the non-existing work of non-writers. A lot of writing writers also find voice in the book. Gilles Deleuze, the French philosopher, posits that Herman Melville's Bartleby was in character similar to the Kafka of Kafka's diaries—a type that he called *The Bachelor*. And from all that Vila-Matas does to expound on that concept, I find myself believing that I, too, am a Bachelor now, literally and figuratively—the guy who has no prospects; the guy who says stuff like, *I don't care anymore*, or *I prefer not to*, or *I'll do it but I won't like it*; the guy who is stolid in the daily confrontation with work and workplace; the guy who can write but is not a writer and is out of imagination, or stamina, or patience, or love, or libido, or money, or whatever it takes to be able to *really* write; the guy who is alone and who walks the streets looking down or looking up but never looking sideways. I feel I can't write. I can't write but I write. What a fucking paradox! I write on my office laptop, after reading some inspiring passage from a book, any book. I write hiding in my cubicle. I write, but still I'm The Bachelor, I'm convinced of that much. And my writing will not amount to much, and even if it does, it won't matter. I'm dealing with the world with one face and excreting it as words through the asshole of my mind.

When I get tired of all this or of thinking of all

this, I try to write a poem. I keep them short, very short. The one that I wrote a few minutes back reads like this:

You flowed out of my eyes last night
And mixed with the air in this city.
Now I look for those lungs you might have touched,
Those leaves you might have tended,
Those clouds you might have blown.

Tomorrow it will rain,
And I will drink you again.

A Small Critique of Capitalism

I lost her, or she lost me, or we lost each other because of our professions. It's just the way capitalism operates. It commands us to fully enjoy our lives, while insinuating all the time that this enjoyment is deserved only when we participate, only when we seek a critical part of our overall search for meaning and fulfillment in the work we do in corporations. Five days of work, two days of enjoyment, and love in the little wrinkles of time that may not have been smoothed. And then the near-dystopian clichés like *Thank God it's Friday*, or *It's Saturday night, yay!* or *Damn, it's Monday again*, or *There is a feeling that bisects happiness and sadness, and it's called Wednesday*, et cetera. Our professions led us to different cities, separated us for weeks, sometimes months, and with all that distance she realized that it was okay to be distant, that there were better places in the world, or better lives to live. All along, the injunction to enjoy led us, or rather her, to different people, which is to say men. Though I'm not sure of the last part.

What does it make me feel? It makes me want to write. It makes me want to write a novel in which the protagonist is our unborn son, trying to locate that paradise where there is no injunction to make the most out of this one life, and where people don't find it impossible to love someone more than themselves, even if for a day or two.

Perhaps, if I were to write this novel, it would end up being about the impossibility of love. Which is funny because in the book *Bartleby and Co.*, the narrator calls himself a *non-writing writer* who nevertheless once wrote—twenty-five years back, as he says—a novel on the impossibility of love. Has some of him drifted into me? Perhaps yes, but there are extra shades here. And as for the novel, I'll definitely add more shades to the protagonist. I will make our unborn son a Marxist.

She

She is somewhere in the world, vacationing. I cannot think of her doing anything but vacationing. And I've just received a message from her:

```
Why do you ask me if I still love
u? That's nt relevant anymore. And
yes, you can visit me in Interlaken.
As a friend.
```

The Bachelor Incarnate

As I'm as yet not used to either, my love handles get scratches from the doorknobs in my flat. In the cramped bathroom the two translucent buckets swallow my shower space, and get filled with dirty, soapy water. In the bedroom there is a thin full-length mirror to which I sometimes present my body sideways, to examine the delta in the radius of my incipient belly. A Royal Stag quarter bottle serves as an ashtray, its narrow mouth demanding extreme concentration. Another Royal Stag bottle with liquor inside awaits, always. There are metal grills covering the three sliding windows in the flat, and sometimes pigeons camp in these overnight and make a ruckus that disturbs the narratives of my dreams. Roberto Bolaño's *2666* lies on the armrest of the sofa closest to the main door; its terrorizing cover always raised at a forty-five angle. And from the first exposed page, Bolaño's emaciated face looks up at the ceiling, with nothing to say, nothing at all, except that literature is its own abyss, which is in fact more nothing than nothing. The flush in the tiny toilet is kaput and water keeps dripping into the commode at all times, and at night this dripping acquires the sound of liquid doom. In the kitchen the only piece of cutlery is a knife and the only things the knife has ever cut are three out of four mangoes that were bought too early in the season. The refrigerator hums all the time, like a hibernating demon waiting for a fool to break the spell of entrapment. Inside it lie a rotten mango and a container of food that was ordered a week back and remains untouched; the rice inside the container must be hard as it must have been before boiling. There is a laptop on the bed, used for pornography and writing, porn that never gets me up and writing that never fails to take me down. Now the laptop has a virus that has corrupted all the word files, which is to say all the stories that are still unfinished, and I can't help but have mixed feelings about this. I'm roaming around in the flat, naked; this man is me, and he has no clue why he sometimes roams inside the flat, scratching and scribbling, pulling his pubes and spreading them all across the floor, getting scratches on his virgin love handles, ever ever ever convinced that he can't write, and still writing.

Psychiatrist

Of course I've seen a psychiatrist. She's a lady in her thirties. She lives alone. She calls her subjects (or objects?) to her house. I see some irony in the fact that she's divorced. I must say that she, with a spunky bob-cut and in a light-coloured top and linen pants, is quite attractive. And chirpy. I'm not a psychoanalyst, she says often, I'm a psychiatrist. Or maybe she says that she is not a psychiatrist but a psychoanalyst. I don't know. She did explain the difference between the two to me once, but I've forgotten. Anyhow. I sometimes fear that, more than listening to my afflictions and remedying them, her agenda is to seduce me. The first time I met her (the psychiatrist), it was about nightmares after losing her (my love). Recently I've met her for loss. That I would choose nightmares over loss is not saying much. She told me that if my nightmare ever came true, that is, if ever I were to separate from her (my love), the greater loss would be hers (my love's). I think this was her (the psychiatrist) trying to manipulate me into health. There is really no way to convince me now that the greater loss has been hers (my love's).

In our last session, the attractive psychiatrist told me that I'm neurotic—that I'm neurotic about my love and my writing. Neurosis is not a bad thing in itself, she tells me. Everyone is neurotic, she adds. Can you tell me what she, my love, is neurotic about? I ask her. Maybe happiness, maybe she is neurotic about the abstract concept of happiness, she says. I mull over this. It seems right, so right that it makes me visibly disconcerted. To save myself, I ask her, what are you neurotic about? The psychiatrist laughs. She's really pretty when she laughs. She says, I'm neurotic about neuroses, maybe. That's complicated, I say in a funny vein, but in truth I'm now thinking about the infinite loop of neuroses. The bad, mad infinity of it. I ask her if I need therapy or medication. Yes, you need some help, she says. I don't know why but I sense some malice in this statement, or maybe I sense a lie. The room constricts a bit. Is it possible to live with neurosis, I ask her. Yes, she says. But it needs to be kept in check, she adds. Okay, I say, somehow disbelieving everything she has said, and then I rise from the tiny designer ottoman that I'm sitting on. I look at her, sitting on a couch with a question in her grey-black eyes. I don't wait for the answer to come to me. I walk toward the door that will take me out of her living room, out of her house, out onto the street. As I'm leaving she asks, will you come next Sunday? I'll let you know, I reply. It's nice to see you, she says. I leave.

I don't go the next Sunday, or the next. Which is to say that now I'm living with unchecked neurosis. Of love and literature.

I walk on the street and I see unhappy men and

I think many things. I think that all these men and all this unhappiness are my creation. And I think, how can all this, this passing by unhappy men on Mumbai's streets, be made literature? And I think, how will someone neurotic about happiness react to all this unhappiness on the street?

Maybe she'll just leave Mumbai.

A Portrait of The Bachelor as a Symbolic Man

The Bachelor as a symbol of dysfunctional individuality. The Bachelor as a castrated revolutionary. The Bachelor as an empty gesture to literature's status of being a sword in a nuclear war. The Bachelor as an indicator of the tenuous tenability of sexual love. The Bachelor as a fatherless figure, and a figure that will never be a father. The Bachelor as a paean to the project of scribbling without a cause and without a centre. The Bachelor as a slave to enjoyment. The Bachelor as a signifier of the successive erosion of all that was virtuous in the abstraction of twentieth-century youth. The twenty-first-century Bartlebyan Bachelor, who does not prefer not to anymore, but who just can't, and still does. The Bachelor as the last generation that might still make it right—it being the world and all the love in the world. The Bachelor who faces a wall so big that the only way he can see through it is by closing his eyes. The Bachelor to whom history is the correlation between infinite independent variables, very similar to the present, and as impossibly vitreous.

Another Day at Work

I'm in my cubicle and I'm building a model that tracks the correlations between lead and lag measures and I'm fantasizing a bit as I do that. I'm using fantasy as a cunctation simply because there is no deadline, which is simply because the task is considered so path-breaking that my boss's idea is to allow me a stress-free working environment. If my rising up from my seat and going to my boss's cabin and confronting him is a lead measure, how would it correlate with the lag measure of he losing his cliché-spewing face for the first time ever in his life? Not much. Because the lead measures are unrealistic. The idea of tracking lead measures is to track actionables and not fantasies. Although *actionables* is not even a real English word while *fantasies* is.

Suddenly an unrelated thought comes to me, which I write down in words:

Interred deep within the labyrinth of my inner life is a masterpiece, though I shall require a talent as good as an oil rig to make it gush forth, and even then my broken imagination may prove to be that faulty little part, that worn-out safety-valve, that allows everything to spill and burn, and then all we would have would be the silent ashes of my masterpiece, though that shouldn't bother me much, for floating ashes are what all masterpieces end up as.

I sigh when I read my thought. I close my eyes and press my eyelids and tears come to my closed eyes because I realize that every anguish of mine is in words; I'm such a compulsive archivist of myself.

I Think of Interlaken

At best, a short story can only approach perfection, never attain it. A novella has to be perfect. A novel has to be a sprawling mess. I am thinking of these things as I walk around my neighbourhood in Mumbai. The streets are wet from monsoon showers, which abated only half an hour ago. Growling autorickshaws find their way through puddles, sometimes splashing water, and I hop and skip to avoid being at the receiving end. But this is a futile exercise, so I tell myself to just walk, unmindful of how dirty I get. I am walking because … because after months of separation she has invited me to visit her. In Interlaken. As a friend. And so I am thinking of Interlaken as well. I resolve to only write novellas. On the street I see seven kids, all around twelve or thirteen years of age, all dressed in spotless white pyjamas. But then I notice that these are not pyjamas. The kids are returning from an evening judo class. They all have yellow silk belts around their waists. I don't know why but I think of an elite squad of preteen assassins, out to execute the enemies of the state. Executing through a judo kick delivered right in the middle of the chest. Then I think of Interlaken. In. Ter. La. Ken. It sounds like a resort town preferred by high ranking German army officers during the Second World War. German army officers and SS officials and officers of the dreaded Einsatzgruppen. I imagine Field Marshal Gerd von Rundstedt sitting in a resort in Interlaken, sitting by the window in his second- or third-floor room, a glass of cognac in one hand and a thick cigar in the other.

My vision of him dissolves in the smoke that he exhales, or probably in the exhaust of the autorickshaw in front of me. For folks like me, closet leftists who nevertheless spend five or six days a week serving liberal capitalism, lunch time conversations with colleagues are unbearably painful. To deflect all the showy, *strong-economy* talk, I sometimes take to invoking conversations about personal matters, for people are more genuine when they talk about their lives. With colleagues who are somewhat closer to me (not including M), I talk of her. I tell them tales from our time together. Of our many vacations in the Himalayas. I tell them of the beauty of trudging a rhododendron forest, of finding a way through the knotty stems of those trees, till all of a sudden the edge of the forest is reached and a majestic meadow or a majestic mountain or a majestic valley unveils itself before your eyes. None of my colleagues have travelled as much and as adventurously as I used to do with her, which I find as something to be proud of; but as I tell them these stories I also realize that I am not that person anymore, that since the day she left me nine months ago I have not travelled anywhere. Some days back, I sent her a message. It was in reply to this message that she invited me to visit her in Interlaken, just like that. Then, three days back, on her birthday, I sent her another message. In her reply, she told me she was happy to have a job in Interlaken because it meant that she got to ski every other day. She also told me that she was currently reading *Life and Fate* by Vasily Grossman. In my reply, I congratulated her on getting the job but abstained from answering if I would visit her in Interlaken. I also thought of asking her if Grossman, in his epic book that was, as far as I knew, about the persecution of Jews in Ukraine and Russia after the initial victories of the Germans—I thought of asking her if Grossman had made any mention of Field Marshal Gerd von Rundstedt. If we were still together I would have asked this question without giving it a thought, and then we would have taken on independent studies about the lives of the key generals of the Third Reich, just for fun, and for a month or so we would have told each other stories of these generals before going to bed and making love. This would have continued till we took to some other historical fancy: about the gradual but necessary adoption of potatoes as a staple dietary item in pre-revolution France; or about how the losses in the Crusades might have eventually led Europe to the Renaissance; or about the horrors of trench warfare in World War I; or about the story of the integration of various princely states into India. Eventually I did not ask her about von Rundstedt in my reply, for I thought that it would have looked less like a question and more like a reference to old days. I instead asked her to treat herself to a glass of wine in my name, and promised that I would do the same. It has been three days since her birthday and I haven't had that glass of wine yet. Maybe I will have it tonight.

I realize that I have walked quite far. There is thunder; it is going to rain again. No matter, I tell myself. I will keep on walking. I will keep on walking till my walking becomes a short story. There can be no rules in writing. A short story can be a sprawling mess too. I imagine making love to her on her cozy bed in Interlaken, a grey September light drifting in from the windows. We are making love after having seen a beautiful Chinese movie that I downloaded in India and took to her in Switzerland. Will it be raining like it is now? I am distracted by a street dog following me, who moans miserably and makes me want to kick it in the ribs. I turn to deliver the kick, but just then the dog gives up and goes away. I find myself on a road that I can't quite remember turning to. Perhaps I am looking for a reason to not go to Interlaken. Perhaps I am looking for a reason to go to Interlaken. Then I remember Pattaya, and what a colleague of mine had once told me about the place. About its possibilities for bodily pleasure, and how that bodily pleasure may ease any spiritual conundrums. Maybe I will go to Pattaya instead of Interlaken. Maybe I will write down my experiences in that place, a novella or something. I am on a broad road which could be a highway. It is a highway. It is raining on the highway and an autorickshaw speeds past me. Shrouded in the rain, the auto is like an arrow of misery. I think of von Rundstedt again and I feel like crying. He did survive the war, and he did survive the initial burst of anger from the Allies. He was required to attend the Nuremberg trials only as a witness. But they got him eventually, for a crime against humanity that he overlooked if not abetted. Rundstedt had to serve prison for a few years, I don't remember how many. After that he died of a congested heart caused by the edemas he had developed in his lungs from excessive smoking.

I leave the highway and walk into a smaller road. I am as wet as I can be and I am craving a cigarette. In the four–five days I spend in Pattaya I will write a masterpiece that will stand the test of time, a masterpiece about love, about the miseries of love in our century. It is for this that I will go to Pattaya. Or maybe I will go to Interlaken, revive a love that may still be revived. In Interlaken we will watch Chinese movies together, she and I, and then we will probably make love, not out of love but out of nostalgia, and after we have spent ourselves we will talk about generals and war criminals, of China and global warming, of the ethics of making foie gras, et cetera. If this happens I will end up with an Interlaken novella, which I would have written in the nights while she slept peacefully beside me. A Pattaya novella or an Interlaken novella, that's a question. But will she retract her invitation just as casually as she made it? If I go to Pattaya, will she never talk to me again, even as sparingly as she does now, especially after she reads the Pattaya novella? Will she identify me with the protagonist and know the monsters that the two are (or will be)? As I walk on, pensive or maybe distraught, the rain lessens gradually and gradually comes to a stop. I am now scared, not only because the roads are empty … I regret having thought of Pattaya. I should probably go to Interlaken. I should find her there and plead my case. My case of what? My case of immortalizing her, maybe. 'Don't judge me, for it is me who is going to immortalize you,' I should say. 'Love me, because I can write about it,' I should add. I force myself to think of von Rundstedt again. He died a few months after his beloved wife's death, a wife to whom he wrote letters every day, whether from the battle in Donetsk or from the repose in Interlaken. My walk is a truly global short story, I think stupidly. The little lane that I find myself on now is the lane in which our house of togetherness used to be. I bring myself beneath the building on whose second floor is the apartment where I, and my love, don't live anymore. Standing there on the road, I am thirteen kilometres away from where I live alone these days. I live thirteen kilometres away from where I used to live with her. I have walked thirteen kilometres and I am beginning to feel cold. Is this how cold Interlaken will be in September? Is it true that most novellas begin as short stories?

PART THREE

Neon Noon

(1)

My pain is a difficult landscape. Or maybe not a landscape but a map for a larger territory full of the trenches of memory and fantasy. In any case, there is no rest when trudging through it. She and I don't bump into each other here, and for that I am strangely grateful. Perhaps I know that if we met we would disagree about the legends and the scales. It would make us angry.

I came to Pattaya instead of going to Interlaken.

While preparing my backpack for Pattaya—it is actually her backpack, which she left behind in some confusion—I intended to stuff in my copy of the fat *2666* by Roberto Bolaño. But then I discovered my Kindle, my long-lost Kindle, in a hidden pocket of one of my suitcases. Not the same thrill as finding a long-lost book, but there was *some* thrill. And I decided against the Bolaño. I did think of how being seen with a physical *2666* would make a person, me, seem more enigmatic than being seen with a Kindle. But I was going to be a tourist, and a tourist should not bother about enigmas rendered or received.

(2)

From the Pattaya bus station I went straight to the southern Jomtien Beach, riding pillion on a two-wheeler taxi. I checked into a decent hotel and went out for a walk. The thin beach was girded by a curving road that went on for a couple of kilometres. The sea was placid as a lake. There was nothing to note except the stale, picturesque hues of the sky and the sea. Some inordinately white cloud-flowers seemed to be forming at the horizon, but their formation was gripped by the same lassitude that infected everything else. The sun was harsh and the town was sleepy, and apart from old, bare-chested white men ambling about in an ennui as severe as mine, and some water-scooters roaring aimlessly on the sea, and some sunburnt couples heading toward their hotels, the touristy activity I had imagined was notable for its absence. On the other side of the beach road, the massage parlours and bars were attended to by fat soporific Thai ladies who, it was clear, had nothing to do with the business of pleasure. I walked on. The blank effort drenched me in sweat and forced upon me vague remembrances of experiencing similar boredom in past travels. But of course these evocations were phony. There had been no such solo travels in my life before this one, so there could have been no similar boredom. I had only ever travelled with her, my love.

But the exertion did something that was not entirely beside the point of coming to Pattaya: it made me want to fuck. I leered at the suddenly materializing sight of young white women walking beside their boyfriends or along with their families. I looked at their sun-red legs, their scorched shoulders, their sand-ridden shoes and slippers. Then I turned around and made for my hotel, wondering if it would be prudent to plainly ask the receptionist where to find women in Jomtien. Surely there were women to be had in Jomtien. I had been told that there were women to be had everywhere in Pattaya. One just had to ask.

But by the time I returned to the hotel, two hours had elapsed. The receptionist was not at the reception. I imagined her taking a nap in one of the many empty hotel rooms. My desire had been overtaken by fatigue and all I could do was go straight into my second-floor room. I crashed on the bed and closed my eyes and wondered why I had walked so much, what had driven me to walk so much. I considered the distinction between *drive* and *will*—one being force and the other, power—and began to feel some vain achievement at this thought, a feeling that scattered away immediately. I felt the heat settling beneath my scalp and feared that I would get a fever that would ruin my vacation.

I closed my eyes. When I opened them, it was night outside, eleven according to my watch. The hours had fled by. I went downstairs to the restaurant and had my dinner, Thai curry and rice, which the sleepy cook heated with a dour expression, as if he were holding a grudge against me for being so late. I had a pint of beer after dinner. I walked a few paces in the direction opposite to that of my afternoon walk, found nothing, and turned to walk in the other direction. The road and the streets that branched off from it were largely dead, the shops were closed, the few tourists on the road were gathered only around the chemist shops, the streetlights were pale and sorry, and all this made me immensely sad. I could not help but think of her and I missed her acutely. I wished she were here, for if she were here she would know what the best thing to do was, and I missed her because, had she decided right now to go back to our room, there would still be something *to do* in the room. I felt a need for sex and knew that it was not just a need for sex but a need for making love *with her*. Then a dark SUV rolled past, and then another, and suddenly I grew scared. The few Thai shopkeepers and amblers began to look like murderers. My stomach grumbled because of the bad dinner; I was probably nauseated because of love and fear and indigestion. I stopped on the pavement and looked up to the cloudy sky, and then I turned around and took many deep breaths to gather some courage, and after that was done I told myself that I, I the owner of I, would go back to my hotel room and read. I would read as long as it took for reading to get me to sleep and tomorrow I would move out of Jomtien. I would go to the more happening parts of the town. I would go to Pattaya beach.

(3)

That night, *Kimiko and Other Japanese Tales* by Lafcadio Hearn served as a distraction because of its first tale, which was about a geisha named Kimiko and her love affair with a young man from a good family. Although their love is pure, it is also doomed. Kimiko eventually protects her lover from the obvious social disaster of marrying a geisha by spurning him.

The story gave me a big pause right at the beginning, when it quoted:

Wasuraruru
Mi naran to omō
Kokoro koso
Wasuré nu yori mo
Omoi nari-keré.

which is translated in the book as:

'To wish to be forgotten by the beloved is a soul-task harder far than trying not to forget.'

That I did not think of her, my love, after reading this would be a lie. In fact, I gave some serious thought to who it was between the two of us who was doing the wishing now. It was probably she who wished to be forgotten. But was I still her beloved? Was she trying not to forget? Was she finding it hard?

I got sentimental and realized that I needed to scribble something. I picked up my notebook and wrote what is now the first paragraph of this story. Reading it again I feel that it doesn't say much and yet says it all, which perhaps suits a beginning.

The next day I moved to a hotel right opposite the beach at Pattaya. The room was spacious, the bed grand and comfortable. After taking a shower I stepped out in search of a girl. The network in my smartphone was not working; I could not search for 'Pattaya Girls'. I had only my instincts to guide me. I circled the connections between the Beach Road and the road behind it more than once. The bars were closed; it was too early maybe, though it was very hot. I feared a repeat of the debacle at Jomtien. I thought I had come to Pattaya at low season, feared that the business of pleasure hadn't really moved into gear. Then I chanced upon Soi6, one of the many roads connecting the Beach Road to the Second Road. The bars here were open and flecked with ladies who sat invitingly on stools, leaning on railings in front of each joint. Red was the prominent colour, although it was a general prominence that was greater than the specificities in objects or walls or signboards or the dresses they were wearing. My watch said one p.m. I became nervous for some reason and did not step inside any of the bars. The possibility that I was too scared to indulge in Pattaya-grade fun hit me then. It hit me that maybe I just didn't have the guts to pick up a whore, and this fact both hurt and terrorized me.

Why was I scared to take a lady? Did I still feel an obligation of fidelity? Did she really care anymore?

The sun brightened. I walked out of Soi6 and took to sipping a cappuccino at a Beach Road café, allowing myself to indulge in thoughts about her, and the thoughts that came to my mind immediately were from our last travel together. A month-long trip to Nepal, where we trekked non-stop in the high mountains. Even in the serenity of those mountains we had had our tiny arguments, I remembered, and as I thought about them, the arguments, my coffee turned cold and my desire to go back to Soi6 turned into a mini-resolve.

(4)

- On a stony pathway by a stream my foot slipped a bit and she clapped her hands in angry desperation, for she suspected that my socks would be wet now, my twin-layered woollen socks, which she had bought especially for the blister-prone, long-duration Himalayas trek. Her big anger at my little failure made me angry too, and I said, 'Never, ever, be angry at me for something I cannot do,' and then we crossed the stream and I added, 'I felt very violent, I felt like hitting someone.' My violent remark somehow made her feel extremely sorry and I continued with my bad mood for another half hour.

- In a semi-cosy room four thousand metres above the level of Mumbai, a room with a pale solar-powered bulb and double blankets on each of the two single beds, I got a hard-on. She was sitting on the other bed reading *Anna Karenina* on my Kindle, her face wrapped in a cinnabar scarf. I moved over to her bed and we lay spooning, me behind her and she reading. I moved my hands over her thigh and then her lower abdomen and then her crotch, but then she told me she did not want to make love in that filthy room of single-ply walls and with constipation burdening her duodenum, et cetera, and she told me that what she really wanted to do was read. This refusal made me angry and I thought it unjust that we would only sparsely, if at all, make love during our beautiful Himalayas tryst and I said, 'You are never ready for it, are you?' After some time we kissed and reconciled, but we did not make love that night. We did not make love on any of the Nepal nights.

- While walking a sinewy path through a rhododendron forest, where the stems of the trees looked like arthritic fingers holding the mountain together, I told her of the Slovenian philosopher Slavoj Žižek. I told her how Žižek thought communism was due a second reckoning. I told her many other things about him, mostly the provocations that he was fond of hurling at people. It was as if I were provoking her. For most part, she agreed with me in a manner I did not approve of, a silent manner, and I realized her agreement did not matter much nor did it satisfy me much. Then she told me that she did not quite understand how such philosophy can ever help an individual because an individual always has to make do with the system he finds himself in. I replied that her stance eventually boiled down to whether an individual can change a system and I said, 'Žižek is also one man.' It sounded silly to me as soon as I said it. She remained silent. Her silence provoked me and I grew angrier. I did not speak much for the rest of the day.

(5)

I walked into the red Soi6 with such ribbons of memories and also another installment of a recurring fantasy about our unborn son. Our unborn son, my unborn son, the son that I could have had and probably should have had with Anne-Marie. Our unborn son who would have become a Marxist and a novelist, a true-to-himself character who would have traced the dotted lines of his parents' love, and who would have found in those lines a grand idea, something that would connect his broken parentage to the world at large, say capitalism, say the cult of the five-day week and the two-day weekend in which love is only allowed in the wrinkles of time that have not been smoothened, and gone on to write a deeply personal, deeply universal, deeply political poem that he would immediately set about to expand into a multi-layered novel. As I stood at one end of Soi6, contemplating my entry into it, this fantasy of mine made me grow ashamed of my incapability to achieve something as complex as my imaginary son could, though in reality I was ashamed of the simple fact that I was here, that my life had brought me here, to Soi6, where mid-sized capital and mid-sized enterprise waltzed together to present the world's oldest value proposition in glitzy red, inescapable allure.

I entered and saw bars bedecked with ladies on either side of me. Some of the ladies were calling me. 'Hey handsome man, I want you.' 'Hey strong man, how do you do?' I did feel handsome and strong for one moment. And what was to be *my* modus operandi? Was I to stare at this bevy and choose the most beautiful specimen? How indecent would that be? How shamefully incriminating? How obvious would it make it to them, the ladies, and to me, that I was here to fuck? But of course this was obvious already. What was I thinking? Of course I was going to be whoring. That's what I had come to Pattaya for. To calm my nerves I put my right hand in my pocket and clasped the pack of Durex condoms inside. I took a deep breath. I passed by some bars, some invitations. Then I turned to enter a place to my right. I hadn't *chosen* this bar or any of the ladies on display. I had just … turned. This disingenuous randomness (in choosing the bar to go to) was how my actions accommodated the faint strains of my conscience, allowing the semblance of accident and chance to the chain of events till now and the chain of events to follow.

The bar was more like a lounge, dark inside. I sat on a sofa and ordered a pint of Singha beer. A square-faced lady in a becoming red dress asked to join me. I let her. She giggled and sat close to me, very close. On the sofa next to mine, a thin white man was making out with a thin Thai girl. I stared at them for a few seconds, trying to gain confidence from the ready intimacy that the two seemed to share. I took a big gulp of the beer. The girl with me was fairer than the others. She had some pimples on her face, which was not too bad, I decided. I asked her for her name. She said something I did not register. Then I moved my right hand over her back, in what I considered to be a suggestive move, and drew her closer. I took another gulp of the Singha. I was a soldier on a furlough, I imagined. Just then, the thin couple next to us got up and took a staircase that had suddenly materialized in one corner of the place. They disappeared into the staircase, holding hands. In the next moment, my girl put her left hand on my crotch and caressed the thick denim there. The sweat on my forehead cooled. She moaned, and although I suspected the veracity of her sounds, they produced their intended effect. Desire is a crazy woman whose gestures you cannot fully comprehend, but who touches you in the right places.

Within five minutes we were inside the girl's little chamber on the first floor. The two opposing walls of the room had large mirrors plastered to them—the pair of mirrors aiming to replicate the bed and its actions interminably. A dim, yellowish-orange light prevailed, and under its disorienting effect I noticed a stupendous coincidence. The bedcover on the double bed inside the girl's room was exactly the same as one of the bedcovers Anne-Marie and I had used in our apartment in Mumbai. Looking at this strange familiarity, I felt teleported for a second or two; a vision of Anne-Marie in pyjamas flashed before my eyes.

The girl, looking at what must have been a pensive face, laughed, and then she thrust a towel in my hand, signalling that I needed to take a shower in the bathroom adjacent to the room. I obeyed the hygiene ritual and returned to the room, wrapped beneath the waist in the towel and carrying my clothes in my hands. I saw the girl wrapped in a towel too, and she went to the bathroom now, leaving me alone in the room for the few minutes it would take for her to shower. I noticed the heap of her clothes on a chair, the undergarments on top. I heaped mine on another chair and splayed myself on the bed. The fact that she had undressed herself meant that I would not get to undress her. But that was not too bad. Now she would return from the bathroom, moist beneath the towel, moist and smelling of soap.

She came back and immediately took off her towel in the most matter-of-fact way, revealing a shapely body that somehow glowed in the dim light of the room. I lay expectantly on the bed. As she came up to commence her job, I was unsure whether to look at her in the mirror on the wall opposite us, where I could see her ass, or in the mirror to my immediate right, where the ovals of her breasts could be conveniently gazed at. To look at her directly would be to get only parts of the two views. For a little while my desire to devour all the views at once made me lose them all. As for her, she tittered flirtatiously and freed my lower body from the towel. I alternated between the mirrors. Then she began doing the things that porn stars do.

For twenty minutes or so we thrashed in various geometries, the jauntier of our angles made exquisite by the play of the mirrors. Amid the plenitude of views, I managed to notice that the girl had a clichéd tattoo of a butterfly on her right shoulder blade and a similar one on her taut tummy. As for the sex, she seemed to be generally cheerful about it.

But as the girl went to the bathroom for a post-fuck shower, and as I donned my clothes and stepped out of the room, the fun began to evaporate a bit. I stepped down into the bar and paid the manager 1100 baht, 100 of which were for the beer. Then I sat on the sofa and drank my beer, warm by now. The girl emerged from the staircase in the same red dress, and after giving me an impish smile she took to the seats behind the railing facing the street. There, she crossed her legs, and after a minute or so I heard her shout to someone: 'Hey handsome man, I like you.'

I left the bar. Outside it was evening, with neon lights beginning to strobe away the tiny truths of Soi6. A few transvestites had emerged on the road. Scores of ruddy white men, possible customers or passers-by, walked to and fro. A hodgepodge made of the various kinds of music hung in the air. I put my fingers in my pockets, felt the lightened Durex packet, and walked away, humming a stupid Hindi song.

As I left Soi6 and headed toward my hotel, I felt I was in a state that can be described as the opposite of sentimental. I had just been sexually sated, and the exhaustion had left a pleasing fatigue in my legs. I took to walking on the beachside boulevard, breathing in the humid air. But there was something lacking. I noticed that the air was missing the salty feel that seaside air is usually suffused with. In the next twenty paces, this thought about the absence of a salty quality in the air morphed into a thought about absence *in general*. The absence of things, of right and wrong, of people. I left the boulevard and crossed the adjoining road to reach a departmental store on the other side. It occurred to me that buying beer for the refrigerator in my hotel room would not be a bad idea, because I'd decided that I was going to stay in the same hotel for the remaining three days of my vacation. Pattaya was fun, or was going to be fun, I had told myself, and my hotel was a decent one. So I bought four pints of beer and some ham and some bread. The teller gave me a receipt. I happened to *look at* the receipt. The receipt as a physical object. It was a thermally printed, long, rectangular paper, set to lose its print and become blank again in the course of time. … Like my sexual experience in Soi6, I thought—each detail of which I was bound to forget in due time. As I walked out of the store carrying my polybags, I tried to trace the events on that dimly lit bed one after another. I realized that already, in less than half an hour, some of the details of the action with my first Pattaya whore had gone missing. Knowing this made me sad, and the fine fatigue in my legs turned into something cumbersome.

Inside my hotel room I stuffed my little refrigerator and then slid open a window to enjoy a view of the Pattaya bay, and although the view was somewhat curtailed by another hotel building just opposite to mine, I could still see the big city board on a distant hill with its letters P A T T A Y A standing out, the letters illuminated in turns in purple, red, green and blue light. I thought of many melancholic characters from novels and movies who did what I was doing—gazing at a cityscape through a window while smoking a cigarette. It was a romantic thought. But I was aware of being tethered to reality in the bay of Pattaya, where night was gaining strength; and faced with the night and the many confusions that I now acknowledged to myself, I lit a cigarette by the window and smoked it to the filter in short hurried puffs before hurling it still alit out of the window, its red dot shattering upon impact two floors below. Then I turned to my bed where my Kindle lay and I switched it on.

I read a war novel for some time, and as I read on the soldiers' sense of disillusionment began to seep into my own notions of reality. I felt a bit nauseated. I switched off the Kindle and took out a bottle of beer from the fridge. I looked around for a bottle opener but couldn't find any. Exasperated, I returned the bottle to the fridge, for I was never the sort to try my teeth on the cap. It never occurred to me to ask the hotel staff for the opener. Amid all the moving about in the room for the simple tool, I had caught some glimpses of myself in the large mirror beside the LCD TV, and after I placed the bottle in the fridge I stopped and stood before the mirror to look at myself. I wasn't a soldier on a furlough, I thought. That wasn't the case at all. I was a soldier at war. I was a soldier at war, and this was the battle of Pattaya. A battle to be fought inside rooms, on beds, between the gazes of the mirrors and the crumples of the bed sheets. These were its trenches. But then, who was the enemy? And for what land, what spoil, what redemption, what revenge, was it being fought? Was the enemy far, far away or deep, deep inside? Were the whores on the side of the enemy or were they my comrades?

I started taking off my clothes while continuing to stare at the mirror. I took Anne-Marie's picture from my wallet and affixed it on the space between the mirror and the frame. I looked at my body. I touched myself. It was clear that like all trench warfare, the battle of Pattaya would be an arduous, testing one.

(6)

I took a shower and stepped out to get a whore for the night.

(7)

I walked on the Second Road, the one behind the Beach Road, and to-ed and fro-ed for a long time. I was excited at the prospect of entering a place for beer and exiting it with a pretty Thai girl, but imagining the maneuvers between these two events made me nervous. I did not want to go to Soi6 again; that would be too easy. I wanted to try new tricks, new lanes, new types of girls—basically to reach out for new experiences. I finally entered a place called Marie Bar Beer, in no less *arbitrary* a manner than I had affected in the afternoon. At the moment of my entry there were three ladies behind the round, road-facing bar table, and none of them was to my interest, which is to say sexual interest, and perhaps this was the little chink in my so-called arbitrariness of choice. What I mean to say is that it is possible that I found it both easy and serendipitous to enter Marie Bar Beer out of all the bars in Pattaya because what was on show there was not attractive, and must have immediately and surely relaxed the psychic fortifications that I sometimes construct in anticipation of feminine beauty.

For details: When I entered the Marie Bar Beer there were three women there: a fair old lady with unkempt hair who seemed to be minding the cash counter; a fat girl who was too bulky to be in the business; and a broad broad who, although dressed skimpily, wasn't someone I could ever fancy. Clearly, with my notions of beauty accompanying me, I found myself in a place where the probability of immediately finding a *delectable* whore seemed probably the lowest in Pattaya.

I mounted a high stool, oriented such that it let me have a view of the street, and I ordered a Singha. Within a couple of minutes the broad broad approached me from behind the bar and gave me one of the strongest-toothed, broadest grins I've ever seen in my life. Everything about her was broad. She wanted me to buy her a drink. She told me her name out loud (she would tell me her name again during the course of this story, but I can't remember it). At that time I was a bit distracted, because I was revising what my twice-been-to-Pattaya friend—a colleague from Mumbai—had told me about the workings in evening-time Pattaya some days back. According to him, things could be expected to proceed like this: The spectacularly-jawed woman would ask me to buy her drinks, for each drink she would receive a commission, and then when I am adequately tipsy she would offer to be my whore for the night, for which 'rights' I would have to pay the bar a 'fine' of a few hundred bahts, and after which I would have to negotiate the fuck-rates with the woman in private. The whole thing was kept decent all along the way. But precisely because of this very inherent contradiction at its base, where it gave the illusion of decency to something venal, these all-night picks, which were the only picks my Mumbai friend had had experience with, seemed to me trickier than the simple afternoon quickie I'd had in Soi6.

Presently I wanted to duck for cover, for the broad broad's wheedling for a drink was unnerving me and I feared that I would end up spending precious bahts on an entirely non-erotic rendezvous. I half-suspected her to be a ladyboy, which is to say a transsexual (I guess). A bone structure like hers was unusual in petite Thai girls. I ignored her exhortations, unable to say no flatly. I acted as if I could not understand what she said and took tentative sips of the Singha, avoiding eye contact by looking at the street while she whined.

Night was approaching. I looked at the dumbbell-shaped cutout of the sky between the upper peripheries of Marie Bar Beer and the buildings opposite the road, one of which was the famous transvestite go-go theatre called Alcazar or something. The city was slowly acquiring a grainy glow that obfuscated the darkness in the sky. Below, a maniacal music sounded all around, with some decipherable strains of Bollywood music that my mind placed in the late nineties. I noticed that Marie Bar Beer was playing Enrique's '*Love to see you cry*', something that I found both ridiculous and melancholic. I could sense the broad broad relenting, perchance because of the new opportunity provided by a middle-aged white customer who had come to the bar. Across the road, on either side of the Alcazar go-go theatre were open bars with diffused red lights, and as I looked closely at these bars and the activity inside them—activity that constituted bar girls shifting the stools or the chairs or the bottles, or bar girls playing snooker, or bar girls generally standing akimbo guessing which one of the nearby hotels they would end up sleeping in, et cetera—I felt a poetic urge within me. I mused that the insides of the open bars were bloody aneurysms surrounded by dark little ruptured nervelets that were these bar girls. My unborn son, I thought, obliquely. My unborn son would raid these nightly paths and find the burnt remains of his father's homeless poems. Anyhow. Soft red light had become prominent inside Marie Bar Beer as well. It was clear that even the second customer was not interested in the broad broad. This lack of interest had produced a rictus on her face that only I noticed and only I felt uncomfortable for noticing. So much red, I thought. So many hungry souls.

After some time, two young ladies with extremely comely bodies entered Marie Bar Beer, both of them dressed in short black skirts and revealing black tops, both speaking in loud Thai to the three ladies behind the bar, both smelling electric and flowery. These were professionals who had daily fare, no fucking doubt, and the white customer at the bar had even started to show very visible interest in the younger of the two, who proceeded to touch him on his left cheek and asked him to buy her a drink, a request that he gladly accepted. As the other lady came close to me, I instinctively turned my head and relegated her to the periphery of my vision. But then I slowly turned toward her, because some inner voice told me that it was plain stupid to avoid a whore in Pattaya. The lady started talking to the broad broad. I said 'Hi,' almost interrupting them. She looked at me and sat on the stool next to mine, and said something that sounded like *Nohap*. I was confused if she had ended her syllables with a question mark or not. *Nohap* seemed eerily close to being an acronym for *Not Happening*, which made it important that I know whether she had meant to ask me a question or was just clarifying that there were no erotic possibilities between the two of us.

The song currently playing now at Marie Bar Beer was a song I did not know, and mixed as it was with the music from all around, it was quite difficult to follow. I was confused if I should restart a conversation with the whore sitting next to me (she was now looking into her handbag), but then I realized that what I suffered from was not confusion but something way more complicated than confusion, something that didn't even have much to do with the whore next to me. I wanted to enter and exit at the same time. But *what*? Was I not already inside it? Was I not already outside it? Anne-Marie, I thought. Anne-Marie's cunt.

On the other side of the bar table there was a new girl now. I had completely missed her arrival, and she seemed to me to have emerged from nowhere. She was preparing drinks for the younger whore and her white middle-aged customer. She stood at an angle from me, and I could not really see her face and had to strain to ascertain her prettiness and her exact role at Marie Bar Beer. The broad broad caught my gaze and promptly nudged the new girl, who then turned to face me. I found her pretty in a homely way, which was strange to me then, so strange that in that otherwise bizarre setting it registered like a kind of familiarity. I took long seconds to notice everything in her appearance. She was not made-up, had tired eyes, had short hair, two thick locks of which fell on either side of her face, did not look like she had really taken a shower that day, was in a pink sleeveless top that wasn't really attractive, had a faded black jeans beneath the top, was thin, had thin arms and legs, had Eastern eyes, had a short nose, had nice lips, had a thin beauty spot on the left cheek …

'I want to buy *her* a drink,' I said to the broad broad, pointing to the new girl.

(8)

The introduction of the new girl in the section above shames me as a writer, or as someone who needs to pretend to be one. How devoid it is of any presentiment, or even postsentiment. I could not even weave into this introduction the smallest hint that the story, this story, my story, has moved a stage with her entry. And so now I have to resort to this, this naked avowal, begging you to exercise your imagination and create this new girl at Marie Bar Beer as a kind of female presence that reminds a man of some good in the world, reminds him that he is splintered and shattered but can be fixed. What I felt, when I first looked at her in her simplicity, was a surprising *connectedness*, in a way that does not necessitate splendour—and I know this sounds mushy. It was this very apprehension of sentimentality that, along with the poverty of my lexicon and my lack of literary depth, had made me wary of mentioning the word *connection*. It would have appeared abrupt or convoluted, considering the flow of whatever had preceded her entry. That I've been able to use the word now is from being able to look up from the page, being able to look up from the page and think of poetry and not prose. Consider me: I was surrounded that moment by streaks and strobes of neon, along with cheap perfume that somehow fostered the idea that every pleasure could be bought or sold. I was a lover shorn of love, searching for sex, surrounded by the lurid music of a thousand parties. Even with eyes closed one could feel the glitter and pomp in that space and time. She, this plainly dressed girl, appeared to me an oasis of dullness, the quintessence of being un-ready and un-prepared for the occasion of the night, not giving the oncoming night and its injunction for enjoyment any heed, not imposing anything on herself and being in fact genuinely tired in the face of the demands of her occupation. I was beset with a similar fatigue too, but it was my role to deny it then—I was the customer. It was, however, a glimpse of all this that made me *connect*.

As an aside I claim that the best literature is also sentimental, and that there are many kinds of sentimentality in literature.

(9)

She, the new girl, sat opposite me on my beckoning, the wood of the bar between us. She smiled at me. But it was not a real smile, and her face appeared for a fraction of a second to be crumbling. As if her sharing a drink with me was something that could bring great pain. I blinked hard and long, and when I opened my eyes they immediately fell into her dark inscrutable eyes that were like jaded copper coins set in wide cowries; and then she blinked, and suddenly there was a shimmer in those eyes, a glistening, such that in the next moment her fake full smile turned into a true half one. I sensed that in these few moments with me, she had somehow relaxed. I asked her for her name. She said something that sounded like a mix of 'New' and 'Nuan' and 'Noon'. I decided to go with 'Noon'.

The drinks arrived, and she responded with an earnest little nod of gratitude. I felt like pinching myself and waking up in a place far, far away from Pattaya, and although I did not do that, the pinching, that is, I did for a moment wonder if she was really a prostitute. The few silent seconds in-between made me stupid and I asked her for her name again. 'Noon,' she replied, again with a true half smile and a sparkle in her eyes.

I must have looked bemused, must have looked drunk even, and something about Noon, the slow fluctuations on her face perhaps, were forcing upon me an awareness of how I looked. I did not want to look bemused or drunk at all.

I told her my name. This was the first time I had spoken my name in Pattaya.

I wanted to take a gulp of the beer but could not make myself do that. She was now looking away from me, talking to the broad broad and laughing with her, presumably at my appearance, at my bemusement and drunkenness. I looked at her hair, her slim neck, and then I looked down at my beer bottle, at my hands and my fingers next to the beer bottle. Just then she turned toward me, and she was still laughing, her little teeth beautiful in her mouth. She called me by my name, which sounded more like an approximation of my name, an approximation that my mind registered as original and priceless. My face must have forgotten to react, for she then placed her hand upon mine on the table and shook it, and called me by that name again. I felt a jolt, as if some lost part of me had returned to my body.

'You no good?' she asked me

'No,' I said aloud, smiling. 'I good.'

(10)

I

Grand classrooms of that red-bricked campus
Of strange angles and stranger agency,
Inside them my stolen glances.

Love was the daybreak after sound sleep,
Then.

II

First dinner my fancy blunder,
Stale lettuce and no cherry tomatoes,
The restaurant stunned by the contrast in our
skins.

A silk stole slid on her.
She talked of parents' divorce, broken family,
being Celtic, happiness.

I should have taken pause at happiness.
I should have asked her what she meant.

III

At eleven in the night I knocked
And she opened.
I sat down on her single bed, shaking,
Wanting to stay.
She asked if I'd brought my toothbrush.

Didn't make love.
Although when she slept I was
certain that she was dreaming.

(11)

I struck a deal with Noon, a deal for *long-time*, which means the whole night. But this happened after many drinks and many board games that she subjected me to, and also many staccato conversations. Her English was either basic or absent, and took turns between the two unpredictably. I gathered that she was twenty-nine years old, the same age as Anne-Marie, both two years my elder. It was only her second week of employment in Pattaya. She had been a nurse in Bangkok before, and had come to this city to make enough money to recover from a family catastrophe that she tried to explain to me unsuccessfully.

During the entire evening, sitting across me with alcohol between us, her manner was a mixture of sadness and chirpiness, and the conflict between the two was all too visible on her face. On occasions when she could not understand me, she would create an expression of great concern, as if our inability to communicate was not ours but mine alone and was something to be pitied in me. Through this pensive look of hers would sometimes burst forth a grin or a giggle so effusive it would make me chuckle as well, and I would feel as if I had finally found a partner in ridiculing the heaviness of life. This glee would in turn be betrayed in the eyes, those plain eyes that I've described before and tried to make something big of, and although it would be wrong to call those eyes downcast, they did indeed have in them the flickers and scratches of defeat. Watching those eyes I felt I was facing someone who was trying hard to be both a person and a product. This sort of charade is what all of us have to do at our workplaces today, it's no big deal really, but through Noon I understood then that there is a difference between trying to be a product and trying to be a *consumable* product. Noon was not the prostitute yet, this much was clear. She had not yet metamorphosed into that ultimate consumable good. She was still *trying*, still grasping the concept that the prostitute's primary offering is not a talent or a skill or experience, but the self, or the self's physical definition, the body. Everything comes after that. As I looked at her that evening, at her swift and shy eyes, at her laughter that could be both reckless and edgy, I saw that she was vulnerable, not yet capable of rebirth every morning, not ready for the sort of Sisyphean stubbornness (or compulsion) that her profession demanded. It was still possible for her to be hurt. And this fact endeared her to me.

Of course it was not only her eyes and her laughter. That she was more girl and less prostitute could be deduced from other little things as well. Sometime in the middle of the evening, street-side beggars had come into Marie Bar Beer and asked the few customers, including me, for money. I didn't offer any for the simple reason that I never give money to beggars. But Noon gave them ten or twenty baht notes from her pocket, something that I found profligate, because the money that she let go of so easily was equivalent to whatever commission she was making on the drinks that I was buying her. There was another such instance of generosity. A man with a polaroid camera approached us and offered to take an instant picture, and I refused, suspecting that his hundred baht offer was too expensive and involved an element of commission to Messrs. Marie Bar Beer. But Noon didn't let the man go. She came out from behind the bar to my left side, leaned on me as I sat on the stool, and asked the photographer to shoot. Then she went behind the bar, happy and giggling, and paid the photographer from her wallet. Upon taking the photo in her hand, she shook it violently for a minute or more, apparently to air it, and then offered the picture to me. 'My gift for you,' she said.

I accepted the gift, although I didn't know what this gesture meant. Today this picture looks to me a rectangle of hope. Hope for what, I don't know. But hope.

(I do not have the courage to show it in full, to reveal her face.)

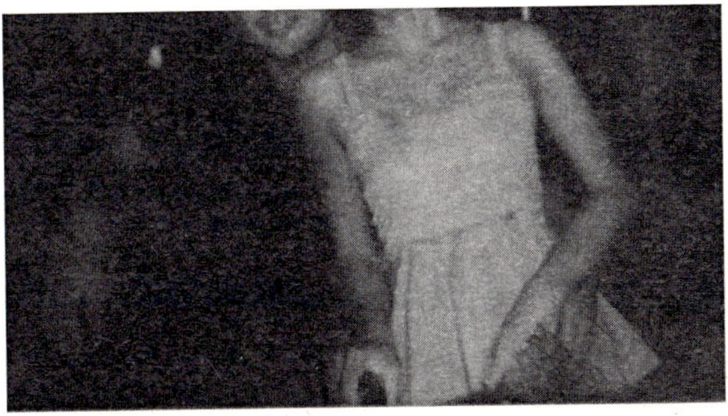

Posing for the photograph, I had taken the liberty to put my left arm around Noon's waist. My gesture was nervous, and as can be seen, I could only let my wrist dangle carelessly about her midriff. It was not in my powers yet to hold Noon. Still, this was my first attempt at intimacy with her. And whether I was a customer beginning to assert his right over a product of choice or a boy simply trying his luck with a girl, I cannot really say. Maybe it was both. It was both.

It was after the photograph that I discussed the long-time deal with Noon, as if receiving the gift had made me want to take her home. By that time the two prettier whores had gone away with the white customers and the broad broad was having a drink with a fat Indian man. When I asked Noon how much she would charge to spend the night with me, she smiled at me wistfully, and for a second the air in my lungs vanished for I thought that she would refuse.

'What you want you pay me. Ok?' she said.

(12)

Our son, *I said*. Our yet-to-be-conceived son.

It was in Goa, the two of us sipping coconut water while facing a faraway hazy sunset.

We will die and our son will survive and then he will grow up and then he will travel the world, *I said*. To certify our absence. To find the terminal point and then move on. How is that for an idea? An idea for a novel?

I hate it, *she said*, I think it is too morbid an idea.

Why?

Because we die. Why do we die?

But he lives.

But he is not the one who exists. In reality we exist. And you make us die. I mean you will make us die.

It is only an idea.

I don't like it. At all. I don't like the idea.

Should I also kill him in the end then?

Fuck off, man. You're stupid sometimes.

Now you're getting angry. There is no need to be angry.

I'm not angry.

You are angry. It's just an idea.

It's a silly idea.

I don't think it's silly. I think no idea is silly. Execution makes ideas silly. By themselves ideas are just air.

It's a silly idea.

Ideas are just odourless somethings. Nothings.

This coconut does not have any flesh. We asked for a coconut with flesh.

Malai. It's called malai. Not flesh.

Yes, malai. We asked for a coconut with malai.

Our unborn son will wage a crusade against liberal capitalism.

Do you want another coconut? I'm going to ask the lady for a discount. Mine didn't have any malai.

No. You can have mine. There's malai here.

We should have as much coconut water as we can here. It's really cheap.

Yeah.

Do you think people in Goa are happier in the off season?

Why?

They look relaxed. In high season they will be all hurried, I guess. Plus there must be people from all over the country looking to do business. That must be irritating.

And prostitutes.

Bof. Why do you think of prostitutes?

Just like that. Goa has prostitutes, you know.

I think you think weird things sometimes.

I'm actually not thinking too much. Look … the sun is touching the sea now.

It's really hazy. I think it is raining over there.

Where?

Where the sun meets the sea.

Is the malai good?

Yeah, it is. You want some?

No. But think of it. A child of Indian and French parentage, without a real homeland. Torn between the West and the East, having lost the only two people who could have given him that feeling of home.

I don't know why, but it sounds clichéd.

Really? Can you name one novel with a similar plot?

Maybe I can't. But that's not the point.

Okay. I get your point.

So what does this guy do then?

Our son. Not 'this guy'.

Why does he have to be our son?

He has to be our son for me to care about him enough and write about him. And write well.

You scare me sometimes.

Are you scared that whatever I'm saying will come true? You're not that superstitious, are you?

I'm not scared of that. You know that.

What are you scared of then?

The way you think. Your thought process. You think so easily of death. Doesn't it scare you? I don't like thinking of my death. I like thinking of my life. My happiness.

Do you think of me when you think of happiness?

Of course.

I think of you when I think of death.

And that's not going overboard?

I don't see how.

Anyway, so what does this guy do?

I don't know yet. But he travels.

Pfft. Sometimes I think you say things just to irritate me. Your entire idea starts and ends with our death. There's nothing more to it.

Yeah, yeah. I mean I know what he feels and what he is looking for, but I don't think I can tell you now.

So don't tell me now.

You are pissed. You want more coconut?

I'm not pissed. You know what, maybe you shouldn't kill the parents. Maybe they should just get separated. Get divorced or something.

How can you say that?

Why are you looking at me like that?

How can you say that? How can you say that we will be separated … divorced?

It's not us, baby. I'm talking about the parents. You are going to write fiction, my love. Those dead parents are not us.

But I told you he is our son. We are the parents.

If you insist.

But why not die? Why shouldn't the parents die?

Can't you see? It's simple. Their death just deletes the complexities that living characters will bring. That's my opinion. Their death makes this novel a road novel. The son just travels aimlessly. If they were alive, this could be anything. Self-discovery, redemption, travel, family, love, reunion, et cetera, et cetera. Whatever.

In my mind it is all those things, but they are dead. The parents are dead.

How can it be about love then? Or reunion?

That's the point. It can't be, and yet it is.

Whatever you say.

Well.

We should go now. I think it will rain again.

Okay, let's go. By the way, just to let you know.

What?

I have just now decided, in this very moment of seaside revelation, that our unborn son will be a poet.

Of course you have, my love.

I think she kissed me then. Not a big one, just a little peck on the lips, the kind that lovers come to love more than the big ones till the big ones become so scarce that those little pecks begin to feel like violent scratches.

We left the beach.

(13)

Tipsy already, we left Marie Bar Beer after I had paid the check and the bar fine. We walked toward my hotel. We were the only two souls on Soi4 then, although as we walked I felt looked at from the buildings on either side, which led to a cloud of terror and shame engulfing me. The metronomic click of Noon's heels on the asphalt was either relaxing or exacerbating this state of my nerves—as in I could not say what the exact effect of that periodic sound was. Noon had put on a faded denim jacket over her pink top and was completely un-whore-like, even with the pointed percussion that her footwear made on the lonesome road. The photo that she had gifted me—I was repeatedly feeling it in the back pocket of my jeans. Not far ahead of us there was the roughly rectangular cutout of the Beach Road wherein I could note a lot of frenetic activity—little organisms of light and desire rushing in and out of the shape, as if a movie accidently shot had been put on display on a minuscule screen. Had someone been looking at us from there, we would have probably appeared to that somebody like two shadows holding hands inside a dark tunnel. Like ghosts in love.

In the middle of our walk in Soi4, Noon tugged at me and pointed with some excitement at a large building to our left. It was an unremarkable building that I would have passed by without noticing even in the light of day. 'Hospital,' she said, her fingers now pointing at an entrance flanked by wheelchairs on either side (the wheelchairs seemed incongruous somehow), and I was confused by this till I remembered that Noon had been a nurse. I thought of risking a stilted conversation and asking her what was on her mind just then, but I didn't, choosing to speculate on my own. What does she think when she looks at the hospital? Was she pining for the hospital job? Or was her gesture more complex? Was it tied to the specificities of our walk, to me, to the fact that it was I and not someone else with her at that moment, the fact that I had taken a room in Soi4, where there was a hospital too? If it was so, what was my role here in crossing a hospital on the way to my … my empty harem, with a prostitute nurse? Who was I? What was I becoming? And who was Noon—a girl, a nurse, a prostitute, a mistake, a decision, a coincidence, a plan—just what?

It was then that I had the first premonition of bad sex.

(14)

The sleepy lady at the reception deposited Noon's identity card as a safety against possible malfeasance. Common practice, I learnt.

We climbed the staircase to my second-floor room then, Noon's heels breaking the silence of the corridor. As I opened the door to my room there was a moment in which faint sounds from the adjacent room could be heard. Sounds of love-making. Noon hunched her shoulders and smiled at me, restraining laughter, as if those love-making sounds were a little secret that we would come to share and laugh about in years to come. I switched on the lights in my room and the obvious was suddenly clear as day, at least to me, and I dreaded that it was clear even to Noon, that there were no years to come. There was just this night, and whatever intimacy there was in that shared hilarity had to be consumed in this night alone, in whatever was left of it. In this room with a king-sized bed, a taut white bed sheet, puffy pillows and two chairs around a short square table. And an LCD TV and a long mirror beside it. And a bathroom with a plastered white tub and silvery faucets.

Noon ambled about in the room for a little while, as if inspecting it. I just stood there blankly during all the minutes it took for her to register things. Nothing about her survey was even remotely prostitute-like, and part of my mind claimed that it was just a natural reaction upon entering a room that one hasn't ever been in; though what was natural was also absurd in this situation.

'Watch TV?' she said, picking up the remote from the bed. She put on a channel playing Thai pop songs. I kept standing still, blankly, as if marooned, as if registering in those strange rhymes a strange inimical poem about the banality of mankind. I was tired. I could have slept. The songs were peppy. Thai girls and boys dancing in plastic glee on an iridescent set. There was something both disorienting and uplifting in the world where the songs came from. Disorienting only for me, and uplifting only for Noon, for while I stayed on my feet, looking at the TV, the songs got her into the groove and she stood up from the bed and started dancing.

My gloom was checked when Noon held my hands and coaxed me to dance. A new song was playing now. I tried to dance. My body's movement roiled something in me and suffused me with a weird mix of feelings. I gazed at Noon's laughter and almost fell in shocking ecstatic love; at the same time I felt the hollow before the onset of crying; also, I fell into my memories with Anne-Marie.

(15)

I've finally found the voice for our unborn son, *I said.*

This was in Kathmandu, more than three years after Goa. The two of us were lying idly inside our hotel room, our muscles still aching from the seventeen-day trek we had just returned from. We were too tired even for bad sex.

When did you find it?

Last night. I scribbled a bit after you dozed off.

So what is the voice like?

It is peppy and nostalgic. Although the nostalgic part is implausible. He is nostalgic for events that he has proof of, but no memory of.

Eh?

Okay. Maybe I want to say something else. It's tough to answer what it's like. I mean tough to attach adjectives to the voice.

Okay.

But it is also alive. The voice. Alive is important for this character. His voice has to be the opposite of death. Because the parents are dead and the son is alive, you know.

Can you read to me what you wrote last night?

Yes, of course.

Is it him talking?

Meaning?

Meaning is it … is it in first person?

Yes, it is in first person. Of course it is in first person.

Can you read it to me in the way you imagined him saying it?

I don't think I imagined him saying it.

Then how is it his voice?

I imagined him writing it. I imagined him writing it in a voice that he must have imagined as his voice.

That's really complex. But maybe it helped you imagine.

Yes it did. Wait, let me read it to you.

Because I have pictures with me I can be nostalgic without really possessing memory. There is a special one—Maman holding me (did I mumble Maman or Mummy in those days?), with some presence having taken the picture, likely Papa, and me looking at the camera, me a blob of fat and spongy bones, me giggling, and Maman looking away, with one hand of hers holding me tight to her chest and the other controlling her blondish hair, hair that the wind is blowing. Maman is perhaps looking at the horizon, for the surroundings in the photograph look like they could offer a long horizon, or maybe she is looking at a mountaintop that we had come to watch, or at a river, or at the maw of a distant valley, or at a wind that she had momentarily wished to see. Or maybe she was just being asked to pose like that. How could

I know? One of my tiny hands, its fingers spread like a web, is at her collar bone, trying to clutch at her skin, and now whenever I look at this picture I wonder if our mind archives all sensations of touch, if it files them somewhere, in some dark drawer. And then there comes that moment when I find myself stressing to recall how it was to touch her then, when I was no more than a toddler. At least I know that once you've seen your mother, even in stillness of the kind that only a photograph can provide, there is no other mother that you can imagine. I also know that there is nothing more picturesque than the picture of your young mother.

This is not his voice, *she said.*

Why? Whose is it then?

It is yours.

What?

It is obviously Oedipally charged. These are your fantasies imposed on a character you define as your son. This is about you, not the character.

You mean my fantasies with my mother?

NO. No, not that. I mean your fantasies with me.

So I want to be your son?

You know what I'm talking about. Leave it … even I don't know what I'm talking about.

You say this because you know me. Because you know how and why I'm writing this. No one else can guess so easily.

Maybe. Maybe I'm too harsh. But is it okay for a writer to be dishonest like this?

A writer is always dishonest.

That doesn't answer my question.

(16)

We danced at a sinuous pace to a rather pulsating song, almost in protest against its verve, and Noon looked half the time at me and the other half at the TV, whereas I distributed my gaze equally between her face and the ready white bed behind her, the bed's surface receiving a flurry of colours from images on the TV. I must say that I was happy to be holding Noon's narrow waist, the sense of touch transporting me to benign memories that seemed to me resonant with the play of colours on the bed. I felt comfortable and melancholic and also a bit sleepy, but within a minute or so this resonance became threatening and soon acquired a pitch that began to crush things within me. And I could have gasped, gasped not for breath but for the present, I could have gasped for more of the present, as if it were only the present that I wanted to inhale, and I did gasp; I gasped and bent my neck and touched Noon's forehead with mine, and I raised my hands from her waist and grasped her at the shoulders, her tender and tiny shoulders, but just as I held her there the song broke off to an advertisement, and our embrace also broke, as if it had been hired exclusively for the purpose of the song. The advertisement was for a headache pill, followed by another one for a tampon.

Noon, meanwhile, had noticed Anne-Marie's picture stuck on the frame of the large mirror beside the TV. She took it out and looked at it deeply, as if trying to recall an acquaintance or trying to memorize the face forever. I was standing a foot away from her, awaiting a comment or a question, and for a brief second I even entertained the ridiculous idea that I'd been found out, that my love Noon had discovered my philandering ways with a white woman. I think I even braced myself for a rebuke, trying to believe the joke myself.

'Photo?' she asked.

I scrunched my forehead in response.

'Photo … umm … you, photo?' she said.

'Yes, it's … it's mine. I put it here,' I said.

'Who is she?'

It was strange how Noon had spoken those three words, with an elongation of 'who,' a near effacing of 'is', and an abrupt truncation of 'she'. It was the general Thai way of speaking, its stresses and ellipses discordant with the demands of English. But her voice and her quizzical expression had added a certain signature to those words.

'She is my ex-girlfriend,' I said.

'Ex … girlfriend?'

'Yes. She *was* my girlfriend. But she is not my girlfriend anymore.'

'Aaaa. *Ex*-girlfriend.' Noon nodded in comprehension now and tried to insert the photo back between the mirror and the frame. But it just wouldn't go in now for some reason, and so she placed the photo on the writing desk below the mirror.

Yes, the room had a writing desk below the mirror. It is, perhaps, a good place for a writing desk.

(17)

All this while, I forgot to mention that the cigarettes Noon and I had been smoking and were going to smoke through the night had all been provided by Noon. She had been carrying with her a small leather bag since leaving Marie Bar Beer, a bag that looked expensive and had inside it a good number of cigarette packets. All menthol, all easy for the lungs.

(18)

We slid open the window and smoked a cigarette each, looking silently at that distant neon-lit board that said P A T T A Y A and did the irritating task of reminding us both of where we were. It struck me then that I had beer in my fridge and I asked Noon if we should have some. She agreed. But as I took out two San Miguels, I realized that I did not have a bottle opener. I signalled this problem to Noon, at which she laughed heartily and proceeded to grab the bottles from my hands. She then went toward the bathroom and found in the bathroom door's jamb a groove into which she inserted the bottle heads one by one and twisted them open. Some foam spilled on to the floor, which was great.

With a beer bottle each in our hands, we sat on the two chairs set on opposing sides of a low flat table. We clinked our bottles. Noon took a gulp larger than any that she had taken at Marie Bar Beer.

'Why you come to Pattaya?' she asked.

'I am on a vacation,' I said.

'But why? If you hap girlfriend?' she said.

'I told you. She is not my girlfriend anymore.'

'Any—more,' she said. It was clear that the syllables confused her. 'Where she now?' she asked.

'She is in France,' I said. I didn't feel the need to qualify that she was actually in Interlaken now.

'Aaa. France. Paris. She France and you India,' she said. There were exclamations in everything that she said, and her eyebrows arched even as she took another swig of the beer.

'Yes,' I said, smiling. It always brought a smile to

my face when people showed surprise at the distance in nationalities between Anne-Marie and me. It had always felt like an achievement, right from the campus days when we had first met.

'But how?' she asked.

'We met in college. In India,' I said.

'Aaa,' she said. 'But she no with you? Any—more?'

'No.'

'Why?'

There was some distress in her voice, and it made me uncomfortable. But the distress was probably a result of whatever she was simultaneously watching on television. I glanced sideways at the screen: two Thai young men were talking to each other excitedly, one of them pointing a knobby finger at the other. There was a doll-like Thai woman too, standing perpendicular to the direction of the pointy finger, staring agape at the conversation and also at the camera—a duality that only soap opera occupies.

'Younotell,' Noon said, still looking at the television set.

'What?'

'You no tell?'

'No, no,' I said. 'She had to go back to France, to her family.'

'Hmm. Family. France,' she said. She didn't turn

toward me as she said this, and I assumed that her scrutiny had ended. I was watching TV too.

The doll-like woman was consoling one of the young men now, the other had left the scene. The young man was terrible at crying. The background music strained a single note. Some of the melodrama of the scene had seeped into Noon's expression, her beautiful eyes wet now, concern filling them, and so when she turned toward me and asked her next question, it was easy for me to believe that this look and everything in it was for me too—for my woes too, for my woes with the French girl who had left me after four years together. And so I allowed myself the illusion that I had found someone who shared my pain, or at least understood it. 'But why you come to Pattaya. For lady. If you hap girlfriend,' Noon had asked. It was a question that was tough and easy, correct and incorrect, with no ready answer that might have been communicated to Noon. It was tough because I really did not know why I had come to Pattaya. It was easy because obviously I had come here sex-starved. It was incorrect because I did not have a girlfriend anymore. It was correct because Anne-Marie did smog my world, still. I could say that I had come here to forget her. I could say that I had come here to remember her. I could say that I had come here to hate her. I could say that I had come here to love her. Or I could say that I had come here to be free from the verbs—love, hate, forget, remember. Everything I said would be true, like in the universe above and around and within us, where matter and dark matter, supernovas and black holes, constellations and dust, whales and amoebas, winds and machines, memories and polymers, fantasies and freckles, coexist.

And so I did not answer Noon's question—which made her concentrate on the soap opera, the intensity of her face mitigated a bit, her beer almost done. I stopped thinking about the meaning of the question for me and thought instead of the reason why Noon could have asked it. Why was she concerned by my being in Pattaya? Why was she disappointed—if she was—by it? She knew now that I was a man who had known love, who had lived it. Did she think it was immoral for such a man to be in Pattaya, seeking ladies? Was Pattaya, in her mind, only a haven for the never-loved ones? Had I disappointed her?

Maybe it was all in my head. A sweet puzzle, nevertheless, to imagine that by being in Pattaya I had betrayed an expectation that could never have been built had I not come here.

'Do you want more beer?' I asked Noon. She nodded, and I proceeded to do with the two Singhas what Noon had done with the two San Miguels.

When I handed her a Singha she jerked up from her chair and gave me a peck on the cheek. Then she went on to pick up Anne-Marie's photo from the writing desk. While being amused at that moment, and while thinking that Noon was drunk now, I realized that our photo—Noon and me at Marie Bar Beer—was still in my back pocket. I took it out and kept it on the windowsill to my left. To my relief it hadn't crumpled at all.

'Why she go? She beautiful,' Noon said, stressing the 'ful' of beautiful. And again, sadness seemed to constrain her voice. The TV became louder by itself. It was the headache pill ad.

'Yes. She is beautiful,' I said.

'You no go to France?' she asked.

'No. I cannot.'

'Why?'

'I don't want to.'

'Eh. But why?'

'Because she went there without me,' I said.

Noon didn't understand me. Even I didn't. For a moment I felt like telling her of the choice between Interlaken and Pattaya, that if I had chosen Interlaken, I would've never met Noon.

'You go to Walking Street in Pattaya?' she asked me, perhaps to change the topic.

'No. I have not been there yet.'

'You careful, okay. On Walking Street. You careful.'

'Okay,' I said. I had already been warned about the aggressive ladyboys of Walking Street by my Mumbai friend. But the concern in Noon's voice made me drunk. And what about her eyes that were a filmy wet now, again.

'What happened?' I asked her.

'I hap—boyfriend,' she said.

'You do?' I said. My heart sank. Why did my heart sink?

'Yes. But he go to London. To study,' she said.

'When?'

She looked up to the ceiling, to count. 'Sick,' she seemed to say.

'Six months back?' I asked.

'No.'

'Six days?'

'Nooo,' she laughed.

'Six years then.'

'Yes,' she said. 'He go but he not call me after. No call. Find new lady there. I think.'

'Maybe he found her,' I said, pointing to Anne-Marie's picture, which Noon had placed on the table between us.

'Nooo,' said Noon, smiling incredulously.

I looked at Noon and imagined her with a Thai

man. Noon, a happy nurse. Then I picked up Anne-Marie's picture and kept it on the windowsill, above my picture with Noon. I wanted that photo to be out of sight.

(19)

The room, despite the split AC chugging with minimal sound, had a stale sort of temperature, a warmth that was efficient at producing films of sweat, which it did both on my face and on Noon's. Noon lit a cigarette and added some smoke to the stuffiness in the room. The windows had been shut after our earlier smoke, and all I could do was to nudge the ashtray toward her and watch her alternate between the cigarette and the beer. She was hurried in both, as if she had somewhere to go, as if she were Cinderella and a distant gong had just gone off. It was midnight now, and I had the second premonition of bad sex. I feigned a yawn, not knowing why I was feigning a yawn.

Perhaps my disingenuousness stemmed from the fact that I was really getting sleepy, and that to sleep without doing anything at all appeared to me a waste. At the same time, there wasn't really any polite way to begin. To ask for sex would be to break a bubble.

Noon, I'm sure, saw some sleepy indecision on my face. She switched off the TV and said, 'You tired?'

I knew my response should clarify what I really wanted. 'Let's go to the bed,' I said.

'You sleep. Okay?'

'But …' I said.

'You want me take care of you?'

'Yes.'

'But you hap girlfriend,' Noon said. She picked up the photo from the windowsill and showed it to me, as if presenting evidence.

'She means nothing to me,' I said.

'Then why you come to Pattaya with photo,' Noon said. There was anger in her voice.

I couldn't answer that. There was a long silence in which every small sound in the room could be heard. Noon's argument enraged me, and the rage was a result of being confronted with my demon yet again. On an impulse I snatched Anne-Marie's photo from Noon, opened the sliding window and gestured to throw the photograph out.

'No no no no no!' Noon grabbed my hand. Whether her reaction was really necessary, whether it was really within my powers to throw Anne-Marie's picture out, I do not know.

'She means nothing to me,' I said, my voice quivering.

'Come to bed,' Noon said. 'I take care of you.'

(20)

I entered her, not with ease, not completely, and she winced. She winced, not out of physical pain or disgust but out of something abstract, something related to loss, or negation. I was looking at her; I wanted to be gentle. Maybe she was wincing at the loss of symbolism in this act, a pure corporeal act, whose only meaning could be in the exchange of currency that would follow it. But the loss was not limited to those nebulous things alone. I felt that it was also the loss of the recent present, of what we'd had till now. What was made in the last three hours, girt as it was in Pattaya protocol, had some value. And my little motions on her, my assertion of my rights as buyer, were crushing that value.

All this about her, this interpretation, I had gained in a moment or two. Her blank face: hidden behind the semi-darkness of the room. She was imagining, perhaps, a time when this act had had meaning for her, though in her stare a void larger than this seemed present. Her stare was beyond me, beyond the ceiling, beyond the floors above, directed straight at the cosmos that hold the literature of our past, present and future. A stare caused by some sort of betrayal of which I was unsure if I was the reason. I knew I was thinking too much, and so despite that stare I—indifferent, insistent—kept on. I kept on, sweaty, kept on because I had paid for it, kept on moving my hips, I kept on, a misery urging its own obliteration, and I tried to make contact with Noon's eyes, only because I needed to lock them in mine in order not to feel like a consuming automaton, not to feel like a raging pig, but everything about her was evasive, everything about her was out of the moment. She was made of mud, I felt; Noon was made of mud and I was morphing into plastic, and both of us were worthless, a world apart—one aiming to become dust, the other burning noxiously. And even before I realized it there came a moment when I stopped.

I sat up on the bed and took the rubber off me. This was it; this was how far it could go with Noon. But it didn't seem final, probably because I was not an outsider anymore. I was like a man who has seen someone drowning. Now I was a participant in a rescue. Noon's vacant stare was now a vacant question. There was shame and shock and some coughing. Save her, a voice said. Love her.

The voice was followed by a silence annotated by the hum of the air conditioner. I sat naked, turned away from a prostrate Noon, watching my feet touch the cool floor. Noon touched my bare back with her fingers. I needed a cigarette. I got up and walked toward the window. I took out a cigarette from Noon's handbag and lit it. Its burning menthol brought to my mouth a sensation of plastic. My nudity began to feel improper.

'I nohap sex,' Noon said from the bed.

'What?' I asked.

'I hap sex with boyfriend. But after he go, I nohap sex,' she said.

'Are you kidding me?' I said, facing her.

'Eh?'

'You mean really?' I said.

'Yes, re-ally,' Noon said. She shuffled and sat on the bed as she said it, covering her breasts with the duvet. Some orange light was falling on her face. Its source was outside our room. But it did show me the welling up of tears in Noon's eyes. 'I sorry,' she said.

What have you done? The voice spoke again. What have you been doing?

'You have had no sex in last six years?' I said.

'No,' Noon said.

'And no sex in Pattaya?'

'No,' she said. She had a pout. 'Customer nohap,' she added, meaning it to be some sort of a complaint. This confused me. My cigarette was down to the filter. I crushed it in the ashtray, looking askance at the two pictures on the windowsill. She *was* new to the business.

'I sorry,' Noon said. 'But I take care of you if you want.'

'No. Thank you,' I said, without irony. I was not angry at Noon, and I didn't want to appear obtuse. But I guess I was obtuse. More so because I didn't know what could be done with the rest of the night. Could we watch TV again? Dance again? Do the whole thing again? Could I actually throw Anne-Marie's picture from the window this time? Could she forget her afflictions and desire me as a woman would desire a man? Or as a good whore would want a man? I desired her. I was going to pay her.

In those moments, the room had seemed to me full of witnesses. The TV was a witness, so was the mirror, and so was everything else. The hair on my neck stood up. The worst was not knowing how to think of myself, not knowing how to think of the situation, not knowing what to do, not knowing what to want, not knowing where to hide. To ask Noon for sex and to keep at it till I was done was still an option. But so was asking her to leave. And I feared both these scenarios.

'Come we sleep,' Noon said then, providing a third option. There was a smile on her face, and it burst something inside me. The assurance in that smile—an assurance not of love but of its pliancy—made me forget the awkwardness of being naked. And not just the awkwardness of being naked. It made me forget everything except itself. And something like this happened for Noon too, for she opened her arms to invite me, losing the cover over her breasts. I walked up to those arms, to those breasts, to her. We lay in an embrace, clasping each other as if we were saving ourselves from falling, like lovers on the eve of Judgement Day. I looked at her eyes like I had never before looked into a pair of eyes, not even Anne-Marie's. She gazed at the contours of my face, its relaxing muscles. She smiled and gave me a slow blink that seemed to delete all the sounds. I kissed her, and immediately the tiredness of our lives caught up with us. She battled the slow but oncoming fall of her eyelids, lost, then opened her eyes hastily, then blushed; she blushed, and with a drowsy smile asked the question, 'You okay?'

Me? I was in an ocean of okayness. I nodded.

And then her eyelids fell. 'If you talk, I hear,' she mumbled.

(21)

After this invitation to talk, I somehow developed a strong desire to narrate a story, slowly, and to push Noon slowly to the deepest and the most tranquil slumber she had ever had. I searched my mind for a story. Of course, the deepest and the most tranquil slumber would be death, and I did, for a moment, wonder that if I had a story so powerful and so poignant so as to be able to kill someone, would I have narrated it now, to Noon. The story would have to be sentimental enough to sink the heart of the one listening. And as I searched for this song of the sirens, the chance that Noon would go to sleep before the culmination of my search became real. To me her oncoming sleep was a grave risk to the length of our night together, a night that I realized I did not want to end. Her eyes were closed and their quaking was abating. There was sweat between us now; I liked it. I passed my fingers through her hair, pressing her scalp with the ends of my fingers, the same way I used to with Anne-Marie. I started with a story from the war novel I had been reading earlier.

(22)

I told her the story of a lone soldier, left behind by his company and hiding in a trench. At one point, a wounded enemy soldier fell inside, and the first soldier, terrified as he was, pushed his bayonet inside the enemy. He then looked at the identification papers and family pictures of the other man. Looking at these, he was suddenly overcome with pity and remorse. He asked the enemy for forgiveness, calling him his comrade. He promised to take care of his family, promising to send them money after the madness of war was over.

The man died in the soldier's arms, amidst the sodden, rat-infested earth of the trench.

In my arms, I, too, felt Noon's dead weight. The crumples of the bed sheet surrounded us.

(23)

In all likelihood, my narration of the story was a dishonest one. But whether I had severely disfigured the narrative—appended it with details or subtracted a thing or two—it did not matter to me then.

Another thing that did not matter was whether Noon understood it. It sufficed that she cared for it long enough. Had she grappled to derive any meaning from it—I do not know. What I do know is that even under the fog of sleep, she had stayed with it, perhaps till the very end.

Which brings me to the question of this story, the larger story that you are reading: Is the fidelity of its retelling a concern worth mentioning? Were Noon's eyes really the kind of fixation that I have made them to be? Did those eyes really have the grammar that I have fallen back to so readily and so frequently to suggest what was on her mind on different occasions? Or are those eyes rendered through my text as an exposition of my own wishes in those moments? Am I projecting my projections through Noon? Am I making a collage of twice-projected images and feelings, all to make it a story?

I cannot answer these questions, they are too complex. But what I can say with honesty is that whenever I sat down to write pieces of this story, pieces where Noon made an appearance, the memory of her eyes spoke the loudest to me.

In other words: Her eyes are sentences to me; I am serving the sentences of her eyes. In other words: I am in a sort of prison, serving sentences, the walls are made of memory, the floor and the ceiling made of imagination. It is but a prison of contentment. In other words: I am naked; Noon is unknowable.

(24)

I was woken up in the morning by a clatter from the bathroom. When I stepped in to check on Noon, I found that she was dressed, all ready to leave, applying makeup. She looked at me and we acknowledged each other. She had tired eyes, conveying some sullenness, even irritation. It hurt me to see those eyes, their fatigue, their hurry, their eyeliner. It hurt me to sense that she was already archiving last night as a silly happenstance that her position and her profession would not allow very often.

I wanted to stop her, but of course there was no way to.

She came up to my naked, standing self and for

a moment I thought she would kiss me on the lips. She didn't. I still had to pay her, and for a flash it entered my head that she hadn't really done anything with me to deserve any money. But I knew better not to take that direction. At the same time, I did not have it in me to ask her how much she wanted to be paid, for that too would have lessened the possibility of genuineness in our interaction. She was a whore who needed to be paid, and she was a girl who needed to be respected. I was the naked pervert and the bashful boy.

But there she was in front of me, a large fake smile belying the fatigue on her face, her expression not yielding any more meaning than the simple demand for a wage.

So I went to the far side of the bed to take my wallet from the jeans lying there. I gave her a thousand baht.

'Five hundred more?' she asked, pointing with her fingers.

I gave her five hundred more.

'You beautiful man, I like you,' she said, and kissed me on the cheek. I put on the jeans I was holding in my hands. 'I go now,' she said.

'Okay,' I said.

'You take care, ein?'

'Yes, I will. You too. Take care.'

She made for the door. But then she turned and looked at me. Don't let her go, the voice said again.

'I very happy,' she said, 'if you come to Marie Bar again.'

'Okay.'

'I hap to go. You understand, right?'

'But what do you have to do in the morning?' I asked.

'I hap to work.'

She didn't have to work. No whore works in the morning, not even in Pattaya. Or maybe they do something else in the day.

'Okay,' I said.

'But you come, okay?' she said. 'You come after three p.m.' I was noncommittal, silent. She walked up to me. 'You come?'

Those eyes were beseeching me. And yet, they had in them enough dignity to not let me feel the master. They wanted me to come, and yet they knew that life would go on if I did not come. 'I will,' I said.

She touched me on my arm, as if consoling me. Then she turned and left the room, her footwear making desolate sounds on the floor.

(25)

The day that Anne-Marie left me was a hot October day in Mumbai. We woke up and had our breakfast.

I do not remember whether we had made love the previous night, and I do not remember whether we made love on that last day. It is likely we did. It is possible we did not. She was the sort of person who would not get the sentimental significance of making love on that last day. And because she would be ignorant of such significances, I had, over time, taken the habit of trying to ignore them myself. Which is to say that the only way we could have made love that last day was if I had asked for it explicitly.

I remember we went to the movies that day. I must have held her hand there, must have deeply inhaled from her hair, even whispered a thing or two as a commendation or a critique of what the director had done. It must have passed by like the dozens of movies we had seen in theatres over the years. After the movie, I must have called her beautiful, must have told her that I loved her. She might have said similar things.

After the movie we took a long walk through Bandra lanes. We must have soaked, yet again, in the architectural beauty of the many old buildings in that district. The sunlight must have been pleasant by late afternoon.

In the evening, back in the apartment, I remember lying on the sofa eating an apple or a guava and she going through her packed bags one last time. While she was arranging the bags, she put one of them on the dining table a bit heavily. The table cracked. We didn't speak a word about it. My insides were hollering, though, demanding that I ask her not to go.

Somehow I didn't.

We took a taxi to the airport. This I remember exactly. I had planned for the taxi to drop me midway, so that I could join a group of friends who were getting together that evening. I could have skipped this and gone to the airport, but I did not want to sign up for the gigantic sadness of departure terminals. I would have broken down, done something silly. And so when the point of my departure came, I kissed her hurriedly on the lips. She said, 'I will be back soon, or you will come to see me.' It was said in a hurry, certain not to happen.

Her taxi started and she looked back at me. I made the wistful smile on my face more wistful. After a point she turned her head. I turned too, to make for my friend's house. Ten steps later I crumbled to the ground, unable to breathe.

(26)

I slept for a few more hours after Noon left. When I woke up, the first thing I saw was the few remnants of the previous night—there on the low table before my eyes. Bottles of beer, a glass that Noon had only half-emptied, an ashtray stuffed with cigarette butts. I took a shower and had my breakfast in the hotel.

(27)

I left the hotel and walked on the sunny Beach Road. The sun rained down, a divine decree. The sun cannot quash the darkness within, I thought, and I wondered if this line could be used in my writing, but then it appeared too plain to be worth anything. Then I thought of many sentences with 'the sun' in them: the sun was shrapnel; the sun was obsessive love; the sun was the collective luminescent dream of Pattaya's whores, the inexhaustible dream that recurred every day. I kept my belief that writing is first of all bumping into some sentences, and only then making more of them.

The sun was strong. The sweat on my forehead trickled over my sunglasses again and again, and I had to wipe them every two minutes. I went into a massage parlour and asked for a body massage.

The lady who attended me was on the wrong side of forty, and I imagined her taking up this profession after a healthy stint as a Pattaya lady. She did well, and any misgivings I had about the massage taking an erotic turn turned out to be mere misgivings. The massage was in fact so good and soothing that it dulled me after I left the parlour.

After this prosaic massage I went straight to the raw poetry of Soi6, without any agenda and eager to follow my instincts. I crossed the bar I had visited the previous day but could not locate the girl I had fucked then. Maybe she was on the first floor, serving somebody. I realized I would feel less dull if I could see her. I went to a bar on the other side of the street, where I sat on a high stool on the street-facing terrace, on a stool often used by ladies to cross their bare legs and make calls to passers-by. There were six or seven ladies around me right now, some sitting on stools, others standing, all in the same skimpy red top and black miniskirt. This bar had a costume thing going.

Within minutes, an adenoidal, short lady from the group came up to me and began massaging my shoulders. She asked if she could get me something to drink. I asked for a beer and told her that I had just had a massage and did not need another, thank you very much. She screamed in laughter, maybe because she thought that I had just had one of those erotic massages that Pattaya was famous for. Everyone joined in her laughter. I too joined in; there was no point in not doing so. Then there came and sat across my little table, toward the street, an old lady who was dressed in the same costume as the others. She was not one year below sixty. She looked shrunken and friendly, and it seemed that both her shrunken stature and her amiability were due to decades of giving her body to men. She smiled at me warmly, in a manner that warranted a conversation. 'Hello,' I said. She asked me how long I had been in Pattaya. She asked me if I had been to Walking Street yet. After answering these questions, I tried to gain some advice regarding the best go-go theatre in Walking Street, to which she responded by saying that Walking Street was not very safe for a single traveller, and that I would do better to stick to theatres in Soi6, of which there were plenty both in quality and quantity.

After this bit of conversation and a few silent seconds, the old whore nodded to my left, signalling toward the youngest girl of the place. This young one looked no more than sixteen, her age decoded by my eyes that instinctively took note of her skin's freshness. The old whore smiled mischievously at the girl, baring her stained teeth. The girl just hung her head in smiling shyness. I felt the tentacles of manipulation at work; it was confirmed when the old whore asked me: 'You want her?' To answer this question honestly would be to say yes, but something about this girl's perceived age pulled the reins on me. 'How old are you?' I asked her directly, at which she once again smiled coyly and hung her head while the rest of the bar burst in laughter. The adenoidal girl shouted, 'Old enup for you!' I looked at the youngest recruit and affirmed to myself that I did not want to do this. At least this, I will not do, I told myself; I will not fuck a minor. And will certainly not be manipulated by old whores.

'Actually she is too old for me,' I said jokingly, pointing toward the teenager.

At this point a young man came into the bar and sat on the chair behind me. He ordered a bottle of water. The old whore pointed in his direction and smiled; I could not understand the gesture. Within minutes he was offered the same girl who had been offered to me. He refused politely, the politeness misplaced in the ribald air. 'He is tired,' I whispered to the old woman, in jest. In jest she replied, 'Oh no! He can fuck everything. EVERYTHING!'

I could not stop my laughter and looked back at the guy. 'Everything?' I asked, and winked in the manner of co-conspirators. I might have even lifted my beer for a little toast, for I did feel like a co-conspirator: as if this young man and I were part of a community that was doing exceptionally well despite the ruses and manipulations of the ladies.

But as I looked at his face for that extra jot of reflection, I had a strange feeling that I was looking not at a comrade but at myself, or at someone who looked a lot like me. This man was fairer than me, whitish, but not completely white. He was my age, or younger than me—I could not say. He, in fact, did not respond effusively to my wink or my half-toast. He picked up the bottle of water he had been sipping and left the bar. I felt stupid and alone the very next instant. The old whore opposite me was smirking and I could not locate her emotionally. I could not locate myself emotionally. A shot of colour dashed through my mind, obscuring everything for a tiny second. Who was the man? I thought. Did I know him?

To gather myself I began conversing with the old whore, who had furtively taken a sip from my beer bottle. 'Why do families come to Pattaya?' I asked her, this question had been floating around in my head. Hearing it the old whore seemed offended. I guess she thought that I was expressing general suspicion about Pattaya's delights as a tourist destination. But then she understood better and told me that the American or Japanese or Korean or European or Indian families that came to Pattaya were mostly on package tours for the whole of Thailand.

'Pattaya is part of package for family,' she said. 'Family come to Bangkok, Pattaya, Phuket, Koh Samui. They stay here for two day, for three day.

Family come, go to beach, go to big hotel, go to bar, go back. They go to bar, but no lady fun. But some family hap lady fun. Young couple sometime take lady. Sometime old couple take lady. Take lady, take lady, fuck fuck fuck. Three people fuck. Sometime old couple take me. Sometime young couple take me. I like that. Three. But hey, family come to Pattaya ein. Family hap fun in Pattaya.'

Family: the idea stuck to me rather bizarrely, and I felt in my consciousness some sediments of a mindless terror. To disallow that sedimentation was to roil the entire mixture again. So I looked at my watch and saw that the time was close to two p.m. Two hours past noon. I thought of Noon. I thought of Noon because I wanted to think of Noon and because I did not want to think of the man. The old lady asked me if I wanted another beer, and although I felt thirsty for plain water I gave my assent to beer, fearing that having a bottle of water would somehow pitch me closer to that man who was drinking water, that silent disapproving apparition.

I moved my head, trying to shake my mind out of the fuzziness it was beginning to threaten me with. I talked to the old whore about my time in Pattaya. I told her about last night with Noon, how we had danced together in my room, how we had been affectionate with each other. And as I was telling her these things, I was also aware that here I was, in a different country, taking liberties with an old whore, being frank with her. But then what did it matter what I told her. To her credit she heard me patiently. Then I told her how Noon had cried when we had sex, and the story about the boyfriend she told me after that. At this the old lady sniggered, which did not sit prettily with me. I pushed my beer toward her and prodded her for the reason for her dismissive reaction.

'Did you give her drink?' the old lady asked me.

'Yes,' I said.

'Many drink or one two drink?' she inquired, taking a huge gulp of my beer.

'Many, I think,' I said.

'I tell you because you are good man,' she said, 'Pattaya girl, if she drink too much, too much, she cry. This true. She cry and then she no good for fuck.'

I gave a start. This allotment of Noon's tears to the sole act of drinking, and this generalization of Noon's tears as nothing but iotas of the drunken tears of thousands of girls in Pattaya … I was saddened and did not want to agree.

'Do you think she lied to me?' I asked the old woman.

She did not reply. Instead she turned to the teenage girl and said something in Thai. The trivializing, near comic tone told me that she was recounting my story about Noon. Hearing it the teenager laughed and looked at me as if ridiculing me from within the confines of her shyness. I felt cheated by Noon, by the old woman, by the teenager, by the other whores around me, who were all filing or polishing or biting their nails and snorting at the Thai version of my story; I felt cheated by Pattaya. In some time it would be three in the afternoon, the time when Noon had said I could see her at Marie Bar Beer.

'You give money to lady?' the old lady asked, 'Aein? You give money?'

I did not reply, and the distress on my face only made her laugh harder. Some of the others laughed too, and this time I could not join because of my shame. Was it possible that Noon had cheated me? That she had lied about every little thing?

I asked for the check and left the bar in a couple of minutes. 'No love with Pattaya girl …' I heard the old lady shout at my back, '… you handsome man.'

I felt disoriented. The confusions about Noon comingled with the weird feelings I had regarding the young man, leaving me in a flustered state that manifested, conversely, as physical stasis. I found myself standing in the middle of Soi6, looking either way, but moving neither left nor right. Whores from the surrounding bars laughed at me. Then, remembering where I was and what my purpose was, I moved. I went inside the same bar that I had gone to yesterday. The darkness of the interiors engulfed me; I was the only customer in the lounge. Almost as if on cue, a thin Thai girl came next to me. She asked for my name and where I was from. I answered and then asked her the same questions. I ordered a Singha. When she requested me to buy her a drink, I said, 'Wait for some time.' I looked around for the girl I had fucked yesterday, because it seemed important that I find something familiar in this place and latch on to it, as if familiarity could save me. But she was not here, so I wrapped my arm around the thin Thai girl, who was beautiful but not so young. I pinched the skin on her waist. I asked her for her age. She responded by asking mine, and upon hearing the reply told me that she was older than me. Then she told me that she had two children who lived with their grandparents in her hometown, and that she had come to Pattaya after her husband's death. I asked her if I could fuck her upstairs. She told me that she would like me to fuck her but it was not possible because she was having her monthlies. Then the girl I had fucked yesterday came down the staircase, following a lean old white man. She was wearing the same red dress as yesterday. I felt relieved and let the other lady go, signalling to my lady of before to come sit next to me. She did.

'Ooo horny,' she said. 'I horny. Old man do me no good fuck.'

I knew I was being lied to, but her words still excited me.

I took her upstairs and fucked her. The room and the events inside were the same as yesterday, except the bed sheet that had been changed.

(28)

In twenty minutes I was buckling my belt. As I exited the bar and turned to meet Beach Road, a conspiratorial fog began to surround the impressions of my recent actions and I, once again, found it hard to recall things that I had just done with that red-dressed whore of mine. It was as if I had been part of a ritual that erased itself, a kind of possession. This scared me, this scared me like how the symptoms of a nasty disease would scare an otherwise healthy man, and at Beach Road I looked at the placid sea before my eyes, the sea that was almost a non-sea, a sort of blue-green lake, and I tried to pacify my fears by telling myself that my mind was only letting go of things that it should let go of—that I was supposed to forget things I did with Pattaya whores, for what use were these memories going to be. But then what was the point of coming to Pattaya, I also asked myself. What was it, if all that could be done here was fuck whores and if that action was not to leave any trace in memory. This argument played inside me and I watched the sea mutely. A bus carrying a horde of Japanese tourists stopped by me, Japanese tourists of all ages. I thought of Noon and how everything that had happened with her, almost everything, was still in my memory, ready to be played for my mind's eye, rendering itself to the question of Noon's specialty, of what was there in Noon that was not in the red-dressed whore, and the questions seemed too simple and also too complex, and I also got a bit irritated by the loud Japanese who were disembarking from their luxury bus now, looking left and right like birds ever excited by the vastness of things, and it was three in the afternoon and the sun was harsh, and I turned one-eighty to cross Soi6 and to go to Marie Bar Beer.

On my way I saw my red-dressed whore, now seated on the terrace, her legs crossed, and when she saw me on the street again she called me teasingly. 'Weccome,' she said, winking. For a moment I considered going in and fucking her again, if only to forcibly memorize how I fucked her and how much I liked fucking her, but the feeling that Noon was waiting for me had somehow gripped me, and so

I could only smile at my red-dressed girl and walk on. Also, like someone checking himself at the first sign of addiction, I resolved that I would not fuck her again.

I reached Marie Bar Beer and there she was, Noon. She was seated across the bar, next to a man who looked Japanese. It was as if she didn't work at the bar but had in fact arrived there with this man. The man cracked a joke in a language everyone but I understood, and I saw Noon fake a laugh at that joke. The entire crew at Marie Bar Beer, the old woman, the fat woman, the broad broad, everyone laughed at this man's joke, and so when I took a stool right opposite to where Noon and this man sat (the bar was semi-circular, I should have mentioned earlier), it took a while for my presence to be registered. I ordered a beer, a Singha, and waited for Noon to look in my direction. I let myself talk to the broad broad who told me her name and asked me to buy her a drink, which I did. Then Noon looked at me. She acknowledged me with a concealed half-smile, a gesture that I deemed more genuine than the hilarity she was sharing with the Japanese man. That smile kept me at Marie Bar Beer till I finished half of my beer, at which point the Japanese man seemed to pull Noon closer to him. He had his arm around her waist, the same way that I had had my arm around the other whores.

He kissed her.

At the sight of that kiss, that long kiss that did not even carry a hint of being forced, I felt within me the flight of a group of birds, and the rustling in my heart made me turn away. I looked down at the wooden surface of the bar, its brown texture slowly turning into tar in my eyes, and that moment from months back when I had crumbled on that road in Mumbai flickered before me, as if my mind's projector had decided to make its own movie, as if all major and minor devastations of my soul were linked, as if all sense in my life could coexist with the absurdity of the world. I blinked hard and fast to dissipate what could have become tears and to cast away these thoughts, to rein in the migration of the birds of my spirit, to hold myself tight. When I opened my eyes to the world, this world intent on the puzzles of experience and memory, I saw that there was now sitting next to me a man who held a bottle of water in his right hand. He was the man who could fuck everything. He kept a compassionate hand on my shoulder. 'You all right?' His touch was abnormal, chilly, as if something either too close to birth or too close to death had touched me. I shuddered, feeling a need to escape. I pulled out two hundred baht from my wallet, gave them hurriedly to the broad broad, and scampered away from Marie Bar Beer.

(29)

I crossed over to Beach Road through Soi6, hurriedly, looking down, avoiding the gazes of whores. Noon's hand was on the man's shoulder when they kissed. Her fingers were bent, as if holding him. Was Anne-Marie kissing someone right now? At Beach Road I considered going back to the hotel room and reading a book. Read a book and lose yourself in that world, I thought. Read a war, read an odyssey, read whatever. You are tired and confused. You are tired and confused, and you are in a city where nothing matters. Nothing. Everything is the wrestling in your own mind. Nothing matters. Neither Anne-Marie, to whom even your debaucheries are but grovelling avowals of love, nor Noon, to whom an avowal of love will not just be a silly lie but another addendum to debauchery.

Nor this young man with the water bottle, a mysterious detective on your trail.

(30)

I shunned the reading-in-the-room idea for no other reason except that I was a tourist. There was still Walking Street to see, and so I turned left and started walking toward it. Half a kilometre, and the beachside boulevard vanished. Further on, the road was all dug up, and pedestrians like me had to walk on the narrow way beside it. What had they dug for? Whatever the answer, the freelance prostitutes had only gratitude for the works, for they provided them with a narrow channel through which all tourists had to pass. Many of these freelancers clung on to my shoulders and said, 'Hey handsome man, I want you.' I shook my head and walked ahead.

Another fifteen minutes and I was there. I passed a gate that announced Walking Street beneath a large LCD screen with a rather well-animated advert on display. On the other side of the street there were a slew of ATMs ready to arm everyone with the only weapon needed inside. I saw a bar where girls dressed as winged angels swooned around poles, but that sort of thing became a common sight in the next few minutes. I was surrounded by a sizeable population of neon-lit boards flashing the names of various enterprises, including go-go bars—Silver Star and Golden Leaf and Lancer and Bombay Blues and Iron Club and so on—though the function of neon lights was not only to flash names but to mark shapes as well, and as I walked I saw blinking arrows and curvy ladies and fish and birds and lipsticks and burgers and beer cans constructed in neon. It was all strange because it was only the beginning of evening. Clearly the merciless god of neon could not wait for the sun's daily apology. As for me, I was one among a multinational crowd on whose heads shone rainbows of neon, a crowd composed of families of all sorts and quite a few single blokes and some blokes who had Thai escorts by their sides. Their eyes mixed boredom and its opposite and dismay and its opposite and disenchantment and its opposite in equal parts and the look of these eyes was so confusing, so very confusing, it made me feel that I was the only one who was new here, the only one who had not seen all this too many times already. I gaped again at the spectacle all around me, forgetting all about Anne-Marie and Noon and the man who could fuck everything. I saw how in front of most bars there stood costumed Thai ladies holding placards that specified the beer price in large font, how on some elevated glass balconies, near-naked Thai or white women contorted in invitations of desire, the lights on their balconies slowly mutating from one colour to the other; I noticed some joints fronted almost exclusively by East-European girls, whose bodies' *metallic* kind of precision produced a startling effect in combination with their flowery scents; I saw how the number of ladyboys increased as I waded deeper into the street; I saw how some Thai women were unrealistically attractive and how most tourists immediately backed away when approached by these women, perhaps distrustful of their own luck or perhaps suspecting the gender of these heavenly specimens, for it was common knowledge that the most attractive Thai ladies in Pattaya were not ladies. Each joint played its own party music; and, passing them, I could not help but feel hysterical with possibilities. I crossed these joints and their women and half-women. I walked and walked. There was so much sex and so much market, so much flash and glitz all around. I knew it would be difficult to stop at any one joint and not think about what you were missing in the others.

But what of the other things? What of the Thai lady who grinned ear to ear and in the process revealed the hollow formed by the two missing molars in her mouth? What of the grim walking salesmen who flashed their wares uninterestedly, as if they were part of a conspiracy grander than the simple motives of salesmanship? What of the two Thai men who every now and then stopped close to the East-European girls scouting on the road and whispered something in their ears? What of the restaurant owners who tried to woo me by speaking in Hindi, as if they knew me all too well? What of the ladyboy who tried dragging me to her/his bar and got irritated by my terrified refusal, and who then cupped my genitals in her/his hands, saying 'ANACONDA' as if it meant something beyond the sarcastic and the obscene? What of the large white men in wife-beaters who looked pissed as if their football team had lost, and who generally pushed everyone around in the way, including the diminutive Japanese and Korean tourists? What of senile men shaking next to sexy whores? What of fat ladies whose love handles looked like little wings sprouting from inside their tight dresses? What of the French old song '*Dans le Port D'Amsterdam*' by Jacques Brel (Anne-Marie's favourite) that played in one of the joints, Brel's shrieks subsuming the other sounds while I passed the front of the joint—what of the stupendous congruity of the song with the mood? What of the alleys that branched off from Walking Street, alleys that were so immersed in the residual glow of the joints' neon that all you saw in them was a luminescence inside which feminine figures danced sinuously and invited you, you and you alone, with their index fingers curling like a scorpion's tail? What of your mind that could not *not* think of Dante's *Inferno*? What of hells and heavens? What of the various wars that this world had fought and was still fighting? What of the blemishes on the arms of certain ladies, scars and blemishes and burn marks? What of the marks that last night's customers had left behind which had not yet gone away? What of HIV? What of the road beneath my feet? What of the kebab seller's dog who barked only at me? What of the sleazy movies that turned into horror flicks by the interval? What of the void of the dark sky above all this, above me, a void well hidden yet doing what voids do? What of the horror?

And so it was not too long after I had entered Walking Street that I began to feel the octopus of paranoia. I was myself but I was also some other inimical person who was documenting me. I imagined a camera fixed two feet behind my neck and moving in a semicircle to capture my head and the iridescent activity of the street, and I imagined watching myself through the rectangle of this camera … and all of this while I was walking. Some of the tourists looked at me as if there was something wrong with my face, and probably there was. I grew dizzy. I felt like those drugged movie characters who saunter inside a grand fair of great commotion while a background score of cathartic quality plays on, like those characters who experience a life changing sort of revelation inside the fair. I had an unnameable fear that couldn't deal with its very first manifestation. I was floating on the thin surface of horror, one that existed behind the lights and the desires and the sex, behind the works, the games, the charades, the joys on offer, behind everything that existed in Walking Street, or in Pattaya. I plugged my ears with my fingers and closed my eyes. Sex and monsters sell well, I thought, absurdly. The background music of the movie I was constructing in my head stopped. I turned around and walked briskly to get out of Walking Street. On my way blind I collided with many tourists and had to eventually open my eyes and ears. But by then I had regained a grip on reality.

I felt very thirsty. I walked on.

I walked on till I reached the Walking Street gate and felt some peace. I turned to a joint toward my left. At the bar there sat a man dressed in women's clothes, his chest hair jutting out of the neckline like little hooks. He was more hirsute than a normal Thai man. 'Weccome,' he said.

I sat down on the stool facing him.

'Howudoin? You hap fun in Pattaya? Want Singha?'

'No. Can you get me a bottle of water please?' I said.

'Okay,' he said and pushed a chilled bottle of mineral water toward me. The bottle had a straw inside. I took out the straw and took a gulp, but the water was too cold and my throat ached. I put the bottle down to wait till it warmed a little.

And just then, natural and inevitable as these things are (this is my assessment today), the man who could fuck everything appeared on the stool next to mine. He had a bottle of water in his hand that looked as cold as mine, but he drank from it like a fiend and finished it in what appeared to be a single gulp. I shuffled in my seat and looked at the cross-dressed man behind the bar who was now engrossed in a Thai auto magazine and did not seem to care for the new arrival. I could have run away from the place but my water was still warming, some droplets had condensed on its plastic. I touched these droplets, took a deep breath, and surrendered myself to the situation.

'Hi,' the man said, 'we meet again.'

'Yes, we meet again.'

'It's funny to meet again, no?'

Of all things that were funny to me, meeting this man was not one.

'Do you like Pattaya?' he asked me.

'Well, do you?' I said.

'Let me see. It depends on the time of the day. For example, it's nice right now. Evening time. The whole place is abuzz.'

'Eventide,' I said coldly, weirdly.

He repeated the word 'eventide' and laughed.

'With naked girls,' I added.

'But these girls have a certain confidence, don't they?'

'In what way?'

'I mean they are not sorry for themselves, is what I feel,' the man said. 'You know where they all come from? They come from the poorest provinces of Thailand, and they are here to make some money. What's wrong with that?'

'Nothing,' I said.

The man scratched the table surface with his fingernails. I did not like it. But this, the scratching of the tabletop, was my only worry right now. Surprisingly the conversation with him had calmed me, as if sharing words were a proof of normalcy.

'So are you looking for something here?' I asked him, to take his mind off the scratching.

'Yes, and no,' he said.

'Okay.'

The scratching ended. But then I felt his eyes on me. I was not looking in his direction; I was looking instead at a neon figure on a wall. That of a snake, eating itself, its tail in its mouth. 'My name is Orhan,' he said and nudged me. He was offering his hand.

I shook his hand and told him my name. His name struck me as weird.

'You were sort of, you know, pained … at the other place,' he said. 'Is everything all right?'

'Yes,' I said. Just what kind of person could come up with the idea of a snake eating itself inside a Pattaya joint, I was thinking. I also thought of that phase in my childhood when my sleep was besieged by terrible dreams of snakes and lizards and other reptiles. It was an ugly reminiscence, especially at the place I was in. To occlude it I said, 'And you, everything all right with you?'

'Yes, I think so.'

The snake on the wall was blinking on and off.

From my left side (Orhan was seated to my right), three Thai girls approached me and one of them caressed my shoulder. I waved them away, at which they laughed mockingly. For a second I thought that the news that Noon had conned me with a story had spread, that information about my emotional faux pas had spread to all the whores, but then I swatted away these stupid thoughts.

'I think they like you,' Orhan said.

'They like everyone,' I said.

'I think they especially like *you*. Look how they don't even see me.'

'So, Or-han … are you Turkish?' I asked, just to talk about something else.

'No, no, don't go by the name. I am not Turkish. I am half Indian, half French. I live in Mumbai,' he said.

I felt for the droplets on my bottle. 'Uh-huh,' I said.

'You're Indian?' he asked me.

I nodded.

'You live in Mumbai?'

This time I did not nod, assuming that my lack of response would convey the information that his guess was right.

He scratched the tabletop again. 'Are you here because you broke up with someone and now you need to forget her?'

I was stunned. 'Why do you say that?' I asked. It wasn't exactly the question I wanted to ask, but that is what came out.

'Well, you look like it,' he said. 'I have another guy in my hotel with the same look as you, and he is here for this very same reason.'

'It's sad,' I said, vaguely. I don't know why I said that. The suggested disappointment with the world's lovelessness was unintentional.

'Oh, I am sorry. I did just nose into your affairs, didn't I?' Orhan said.

I assumed silence, determined to keep it for a few moments. The cross-dressed man across the barfront tore a page from the magazine he was reading; he folded it twice and pushed it under his neckline. He did so surreptitiously—why, I did not understand. Once again I started sensing a camera behind my back. I felt I was at risk, but at the same time a certain insolence grew within me and I knew that the only way I could counter everything—but what was it that needed countering?—was to risk things even further. It was as if a hole had opened before me and I had decided to jump into it headlong. I realized—and my realization was like the product of an immediate epiphany—that Orhan and I had more things to talk about.

'Orhan,' I said.

'Yes?'

'How did you get your name? There is a writer by that name, you know?'

'Yes. It was … my father,' Orhan said. 'His idea was to go for a Turkish name. Turkey being, like, midway between Indian and France.'

'You've read Orhan Pamuk?' I asked.

'Yes, a couple of his novels,' Orhan said. Then, after a few second he added, 'My father was a writer too.'

I noticed how he referred to his father in the past tense. 'And your mother?'

'She was … she was various things,' he said.

'When …' I considered how to pose this, 'when did your parents pass away?'

'They didn't,' Orhan said. 'They separated. It was like they ceased to exist for me when they separated. I was fourteen then, and had to switch between India and France a lot.'

'It could become a good novel, you know. Do you write?' I asked him. My question made Orhan nervous, it seemed. But I knew there was sweat on my face too. For some reason, I had a flashing image of flipping a book in my mind's eye.

'I write some poetry,' he said. 'Nothing grand.'

I drank the water from my bottle. Completely. Then I ordered another. It was as cold as the first one; it, too, would have to wait.

'Orhan the orphan' he said for some reason, smiling, although visibly stressed, perhaps by my questions.

And me, was I not distressed? For sure I was. Sitting next to Orhan, I had another bout of incoherence in which I remembered watching YouTube videos where animals—an iguana, a cat, a monkey, or even a dog—would confront its own reflection in a mirror and become very aggressive out of pure fear. And then the thought that the world was huge, too huge. The world was huge, yes, and it was futile to look for any redemption, but what was I to do with its enigmas? With Orhan I knew precisely what to say, as if my words were preordained by the very narrative that the camera behind me wanted to capture, but this conviction of mine was also to hit me hard on its return, reflected as it were from the surface that was Orhan; it was to come back to me as fear, because it was beyond doubt that Orhan too knew precisely what to say to me, and this senseless yet exact duality was almost a physical presence between us now, a presence as present as the droplets that were yet again accumulating on my second water bottle, a presence as real as the yellow t-shirt that Orhan was wearing, which was an exact replica of a t-shirt that had been gifted to me by Anne-Marie on my twenty-fifth birthday. For a second I considered asking Orhan where he got this shirt from, but decided against it. Everything seemed to me complex beyond solution, but I was also close to a point where it seemed enticing to give up all solving. To continue talking to Orhan, here, now, as obliquely or as directly as it were, seemed more important than anything else in the world. It was another matter altogether that some of the bar girls had mounted the pedestals and a ubiquitous carnival of pole dancing had begun. The place was suddenly very noisy with party songs. The cross-dressed man in front of us had his tongue out of his mouth, in what was definitely a grotesque form of excitement.

'What did your father write?' I asked Orhan. I had to shout to be heard.

'Everything,' he answered. 'Poems, short stories, even a couple of novels.'Orhan said something else but his voice was drowned out by the loud music of the place. The girl closest to us was massaging her tiny boobs. I was enjoying the scene, my enjoyment both befitting and misplaced, and therefore mildly confusing.

'So your heartbreak happened recently?' Orhan shouted the question to me.

I don't know why but I felt I could not answer the question in a straightforward manner. I shifted in my chair. I cleared my throat. I resorted to what I now consider a poetic response. Maybe a sentimental response. The words came out as if they had been rehearsed over and over. This is what I said: 'Well, she left about a year back. Eleven months, more like. But how do I know just when my heart broke? How many days before she left did it begin to break? I don't know that. The breaking has continued. But somehow the story tore and now even that tearing has to end. I would know if there was anymore to it. There is no more to it. This is the end. Though life goes on indifferently, you know, like clichés do, like truth does.'

Orhan nodded and I knew that he had missed most of what I had said. 'My father wrote poems,' he said. 'Many.'

'Yeah?'

'Yes. Many poems. There is a poem about __________ opening into an impenetrable dark.

________ digging a hole________. I think that one borrows ________________. Paul Celan. CHE-LAN. A poem about remembering the evening sky of ______. And Jordan. He calls the sky a lavender beast. There is a very similar poem _________. _________ giant autumn______. You know what a crocus means? A CROCUS? Then there is a poem about a couple and their baby ____________ Himalayas, camping. A poem about drinking _________ the sky. A poem about protecting __________ from the first monsoon showers. _______ searching for constellations. ____________________. Isn't that funny? I find that funny. There is a poem about a ball _________________a pool of black water where it will probably float. And others. Many __________'

I heard perhaps only half of what he said, but filling the blanks of what was not heard did not seem impossible, nor did it seem imperative. I had a feeling that I knew these poems just as well as I knew myself, but it would have been an extremely stupid thing to say. So I stayed silent and drank my water, choosing to catch a glimpse of the anfractuous girls.

'Poetry is useless,' Orhan shouted after some time. I saw that he had a Singha in front of him now.

'Yes. Life is a fucking war novel,' I said. The words just came out of my mouth.

'_________' Orhan shouted something.

'Yes, a document of the trenches,' I said. 'The fucking dregs. Rat piss and rat semen.'

'I realized…' Orhan said. I told him that I could not hear him, so he came closer and began again: 'I realized some days back that my father had been to Pattaya. Alone. That is why I came here.'

I felt like ordering a Singha now. The cross-dressed man obliged; he seemed to have grown taller by an inch or two in the last half hour. Or maybe he had been replaced by another cross-dressed man. But this man also had chest hair jutting out of his neckline.

'Well, he must have had his fun,' I said.

'I prefer not to think about that.'

'But what do you want to discover here?'

'I don't know,' Orhan said. 'It is tough. It is tough to describe, I mean. The things he saw, I want to see those things. With the same eyes, maybe. Maybe I like believing that ______________.'

'How did you find out that he had been here?' I asked.

'He published a set of poems about Pattaya,' he said. 'Very, very descriptive.' Orhan winked, but wistfully.

We clinked our beer bottles and made a little toast to Pattaya. If we were in the same boat it would also have been a boat in the eye of a storm, a storm belonging to no season. The music at the place suddenly died down.

Orhan looked at the dancing girls, now coming down their pedestals. 'I said the thing about Pattaya's whores not being sorry for themselves. It was a stupid thing to say.'

I immediately thought about Noon; and Orhan's words, which had come to me clearly this time as the music had been shut down, somehow made me feel that Noon had not swindled me into a sexless night, that she was as innocent as she had seemed and that the old woman at Soi6 had just peeved me maliciously. Sure enough, a Pattaya of disguised suffering suited me better than a Pattaya of unadulterated pleasure.

'In the last two days in Pattaya,' Orhan carried on, 'I have sometimes felt as if there is a scream that prevails all over the city.'

'A scream?'

'But it is a dead scream. Or a scream of death. I don't know. A howl out of slaughter. Of something slaughtered by the edges of these neon lights.'

'What do you mean?'

'Well, you know, in this city of pleasure, pain has suffered genocide.'

(31)

I remember most of what was said between Orhan and me, which is strange enough in itself, but there was a phase in that conversation after Orhan had used the word 'genocide', when the distance between the two of us collapsed. This is not to say that we became close in the figurative sense, or *connected*, as I might have said in an unsophisticated moment. This is to make an even taller claim: Our identities became irrelevant. His words were mine and mine his. It was like talking in a dream, or in a movie, where the lines are the construct of a single mind. I was on my guard, no doubt, and a thin curtain of fear continued to billow inside me, but it also struck me that this fear was the fear of a miracle, the fear of stumbling on something powerful, something like love.

The end of the conversation too had some similarity with the capricious ways of love. A couple of Thai women distracted me, and in the time it took me to politely refuse their advances, Orhan disappeared from his position next to mine.

I took the long walk back to my room then, intending to rest, or rather, to enter an enclosure and give myself a break from Pattaya.

I found my room dirty and immediately thought of complaining to the hotel staff, but then

I remembered that it was I who had asked them not to clean the room that day. I had perhaps done that out of a maudlin desire to preserve Noon's presence in the room. There were many marks of the previous night: the limp condom that I had used lay on the floor, on one side of the bed, and the torn condom wrapping lay on the bedside table; two long black strands of Noon's hair snaked about on the white bed sheet, which was terribly crumpled and gave off a weird smell that I imagined to be a derivative of her sweat and perfume; my own body hair was scattered around the room; the two pictures on the low tabletop were surrounded by bottles of beer and a half-empty glass. All these marks just vexed me now. They either pointed at sex or a connection—neither of which had really concluded. I affixed Anne-Marie's picture to the mirror, from where it could see the bed. I put the other picture on the writing table just below the mirror. I then took to looking at myself, at my beat-down face, and thought of Orhan—of how his eyes were like mine, blue while mine were brown; of how his nose was just like mine, only slightly upturned; and also of how his ears were similar to mine, only less protuberant. I then looked at Anne-Marie's picture, her eyes and nose and ears. A poet, that's what Orhan had called himself. I settled on the bed then, and resolved to read myself to sleep.

I read some poetry this time. While reading, I often imagined Orhan traipsing through Pattaya's streets, writing down things in a little notebook, things that would later turn to poems. My thoughts and the questions embedded in them brewed and brewed till they slowly became too much. Beyond the window, on a hill that was faraway, the letters P A T T A Y A twinkled. I shut my Kindle, got off the bed and dropped the spent latex in the trash. There were sounds coming from the room next to mine, and hearing the grunts and moans, I felt that all this literary cogitation was a waste of time. I was a tourist in Pattaya, a tourist with money in his pocket. And whether I had a story and whether that story was to be augmented in this city should be of no concern. What happens to pain is irrelevant, as long as there is pleasure. I went to the bathroom and washed my face. In the mirror above the sink, I bared my teeth to see how a grin would appear on my face—a dirty, whore-mongering grin. All I got was a grimace. Frustrated with myself, I decided to have a whore for the night.

And so in thirty minutes, I was on Beach Road with a whore shackled to my elbow. On my way, sometimes, when I was not looking down at the asphalt, I would look up at the sky. And I did squint for a view of the Orion, the Roman Soldier with the large penis, but there were clouds and the whore was Thai-ly giggling. And I did think of you—NO, not you, HER—and I did think of HER, of the nightly walks in dimly lit parks in that red-bricked campus where SHE would go away from me ten paces only to run back and jump into my arms and I knew again, what I had known ever since those park nights, that it was risky for everything to be HER, and I did caress the whore's arm, did feel the coolness of her flesh, and I did bring her to my hotel room with all the nonchalance my solitude could muster, my efforts at nonchalance true to my status as consumer, and I did consume the whore, consumed even the consuming in the mirrors, from where HER photograph gaped at us, and when I was sated I did try to run my fingers through the whore's hair in the manner SHE, only SHE, knows but may have forgotten, but the whore didn't care and I asked her politely to leave, and after she left I switched on the television and watched a slew of Thai music videos, and I thought of my bed as a short story of surrender in crumpled white sheet, and I did turn to poetry again, started thinking in that pathetic way again, knowing that memory was my enemy.

(32)

The whore I fucked that night called herself Ai. To ignore her role in this story is possible, but it feels wrong to me now.

My desire to get a whore for the night was strong, and I did not have the energy to walk too far. I took to Beach Road and told myself that I would turn into the first bar that came to my left. I did so and entered a place called The Green Joint, which turned out to be quite literal, for the place was awash with a dark green light of no traceable source. There were two or three leftover ladies there, one of them being Ai, who sat behind the bar on a table, gossiping with another whore. She was the most passable face among the lot there. I could have just gone up to her and asked her to accompany me, but out of some vague sense of decency I placed myself at the bar and ordered a shot of whiskey. An old lady manned the territory behind the bar; she was playing a Tetris-like game on her smartphone. After some sips of my whiskey I asked her if I could have a lady for the night. 'Only one?' she asked me, in the tone of tired shopkeepers who are all too ready with a discount when it's near closing time. I gave some thought to a threesome, and if the ladies at The Green Joint had been pretty I would have perhaps taken two of them. But it was not so, and so I consoled myself with the fact that a threesome was tiring business, with the necessary change of condom every time the man moved from enjoying one lady to the other. 'One,' I said, and then pointing to Ai added, 'That one.' Ai came up to me immediately and smiled. Her smile was marked by the blackness of an incisor in the lower jaw, possibly due to a cavity. I could not refuse now, I thought, not merely because she had a bad tooth. I drew her closer to me. I was decidedly un-shy, and maybe I overdid the drawing close bit, for Ai squirmed out of my grip. Anyway, the old lady behind the bar made me pay for the whiskey and the bar fine, and off we were—Ai and I.

Away from the green light of The Green Joint, in the fifty or so paces before the right turn into Soi4 where my hotel was, I could evaluate Ai more clearly, and I realized that she wasn't to my liking and that I had made a mistake. Once again I felt low, and once again, by now like an automatic maneuver, my pathetic mind travelled to pathetic thoughts about Anne-Marie. Ai clutched at me, visibly happy at landing a customer. Anne-Marie and Orhan, I was thinking. Also Noon. I looked up at the sky, as if in prayer. On a renewed whim I decided I would fuck Ai's little brains out that night.

Two things happened almost immediately after we entered the room and I switched on the lights. I saw the difference in complexion between Ai's skin below her elbows and knees and her skin elsewhere. Her limbs were as dark as charcoal, while the rest of her body was of a much lighter shade. I have a rice farmer for my girl tonight, I thought, feeling further deflated. On Ai's side, the deflation happened due to the slovenly state of the room. She used her broken English to convey her displeasure, and if a third ethereal party were gathering cues from the resulting rictuses on our faces, it would have bet money on the night passing without a fuck. But me, I was going to be decisive. I ordered Ai to undress. She did so. Then I ordered her to suck my cock. This she completely refused. 'I no suck cock.'

We fucked despite our moods and Anne-Marie's photo's gaze and other inconveniences, and kept at it even though it was never good for me.

After the fuck, Ai tried getting more intimate with me, as in intimate on a personal level. I had struck a long-time deal with her, and she must have known that that gave me the right to fuck her repeatedly, all night. To avert this, she had to distract me; and to distract me it was essential to become friendly. And so she laboured to take out her smartphone from her jeans pocket and lay her dichromatic body beside me and began flicking through her picture gallery. The pictures were intended to evoke my interest, something that they eventually succeeded in doing. These were pictures of Ai, of her white clients, of her ex-husband, and finally of her daughter who seemed no younger than eight and looked no different from nice, uniform-clad, zoo-visiting eight-year-olds anywhere in the world.

Knowing that your whore for the night is also someone's loving mother needles your conscience in a very strange way. More so when you have seen the child, more so when you have seen the child and the mother together, more so when you can connect the dots and realize that the whore is a whore because the child needs to be fed, to be educated and to grow up and not be a whore. Speaking for myself: As I looked at those pictures, tentatively at first and later with intent, I involuntarily abdicated the throne of being the central character of my own story, one who was besieged with love and reminiscence and a painful addiction to literature, and I took on the role of a supporting character in Ai's saga, one where she had to pass under scores and scores of men (of which I was an indistinguishable part), only to raise her child against all the odds that there may be. And although at the back of my mind I was aware that this, this display of family photographs, was in itself a manipulation, I could not avoid being manipulated, simply because it was liberating to feel like an inconsequential part of someone's story. There was nothing I could do to alter the course of Ai's saga; and aware of the lightness of my every feeling or action now, I allowed myself to feel tender toward her and tried to caress her hair in the only manner I knew.

But inconsequentiality is impossible to sustain. Soon my fingers got into a knot in her hair and pulled at them. She shifted her position a bit, and it appeared that she had no more pictures to show. From being flotsam, I immediately turned into the captain of my ship, a captain who had lost his compass many moons ago. And Ai turned into this ugly whore who was mother to an eight-year-old. One of the many in Pattaya. One of the many that I would forget. The air in the room soured unbearably, as if Noon's sweat and my sweat and Ai's sweat had just concluded foul reactions with each other. I knew that Anne-Marie still smiled in her little photo, her face resplendent albeit marred by the blotches and stipples time had created on the paper, things I could not see from the bed but knew existed.

I will have a wife and I will have children, I thought, and my children will see the world die, or maybe their children will, and my words will burn and others' words will burn and all the words will disperse as ashes in the black milk of dawn. Ai left, and I switched on the TV to watch some Thai music videos. I made vague associations between the various things in the room. My sullen bed sheet, my writer's mind, my lover's heart, the sweat of whores, the girls and boys dancing on TV, the simmering of the air conditioner, a freshly spent condom on the floor, a photo on my mirror.

Day after tomorrow I have my flight back home, I thought. I shut off the TV, drew the curtains and fell on my bed.

(33)

That night I dreamt as if a projector had been installed in my mind and a slew of reels had been fed into it. The reels played not in any order, but jumbled, which is not much because such is the custom of dreams. It started with a faceless woman and me walking in a park at eventide, hand in hand. I can't say that it was Anne-Marie because the dream never allowed me to turn my head to ascertain that.

'Come on, we need to catch the ship,' I said to this faceless woman, feeling a panic of meaninglessness right after I said it. To our left there now was the lapping sea, although its darkness allowed only the foam of the waves to be visible. A ship sounded its horn, and we could see its few lights from the shore. The woman broke free from my grip and ran toward the ship. She splashed into the waves and soon began to drown. I swam over to her, but in-between I was taken over by the waves many times. I opened my eyes under the water and, although I could not spot her, I saw something wholly incomprehensible at the bottom of the ocean, a shapeless mass of agitation. Terrified, I came up for a breath, and the woman appeared an arm's length away. I lunged and held her by the neck and began to pull her out. But as I was saving her I also saw the commotion below us, those warring energies, those indescribable monsters, and something perverse grew within me and I began to twist the neck in my grip and push the head under water, twisting and pushing with all the strength I had, and then there was a gurgling sound, and then a bodily struggle, and then a howl drowned out by the water, and then the growing rigidness of a body, and then its sudden limpness, and a rush of fatigue in my limbs, the sweet fatigue of a job well done, and from my lungs a content, distended sigh. The ordeal over, I looked up, the body still in my grip. The ship had come very close by now, and a rope twirled down from its deck, not too far from me. Before making for the rope, I lifted the body to look at the face. It was not a woman. It was Orhan. Blue-eyed, mouth agape, death-shocked Orhan. I lost all sense of reality, of whatever reality a dream can encapsulate. In a blur

I was on the ship's deck, Orhan's contorted body at my feet. I called for a doctor. There was no doctor, but there was a nurse, who came running toward me. She looked at Orhan and said, 'He dead.' The nurse was, of course, Noon. 'I killed him,' I said to Noon. She shrugged and said, 'He hap to die.' I asked her what she meant by that, but Noon had a hand on my cheek now; she was caressing me. 'He hap to die,' she said again. The next instant Noon and I were making love on the deck, beside Orhan, who was now disappearing into those blurry edges of the dream's frame. I had hiked up Noon's white skirt, and she was emoting as if she wanted me, as if this was what she had been waiting for. Our undulations went on and on. The ship sounded its horn again, as if goading us on. My dream self was still thinking of the murder it had committed. In certain ways, I began interpreting the dream from inside it. Noon was present not as Noon but her meaning, whatever it was. My unborn son, I said, silently, perhaps to the meaning that was Noon. My unborn son, I said again, and the shadow that was Noon encouraged me to speak.

(34)

My unborn son, that bastard spawned in sentimentality, that symbol of an imagined future, that monkey on my back. My unborn son, my sweet monkey, the remainder of a disaster, my oncoming madness, my artistic possibility, my idea of art, my fountainhead, my curse, my terrible curse, the blood and tincture, both, of my traumas, the locus of my rebellions, my Marxist son, my novelist son, my poet son, my absent son, the detritus of my love, the cancer of my heart, my us, my us, my pus—that son of a bitch had to die.

(35)

When I woke up the next morning, tired and with a head ache from all that dreaming, I knew the pattern my day was going to take. I took a crap. I washed my hands. I brushed my teeth in front of the bathroom mirror. I had no trouble with what the mirror showed me, which is to say that I had some unselfconscious moments that morning. What I didn't do was try to construct a grin. I was going to fuck whores, this being my last day, and I felt comfortable in that knowledge. There was the matter of Noon. As for Orhan, I didn't give him much thought. I somehow knew I was not going to bump into him.

I had the staff clean my room before I took a shower. The change of bed sheets and towels, the clearing of beer bottles and cigarette butts, the replacement of the odour in the room with something both flowery and synthetic—all these had a salutary effect on me. I felt anew, didn't smoke the entire morning, and even considered quitting smoking forever. I went to a restaurant that served English breakfast. I ate slowly, and read the first two chapters of an American crime novel.

Then I took a walk along the seaside boulevard. I noticed the tourists, especially the ones who were alone like me. They walked slower than the rest, a bit dazed, perhaps, by how their mindless sexual romps still managed to *play* with their minds. Maybe some of them were clean, had not frolicked with the ladies in Pattaya, but I was lethargic and allowed my assumptions to be all-inclusive. While most faces were impassive, none could be said to be looking happy. That the transaction always left behind a remainder inside, a beautiful ache or an ugly trouble—this knowledge was not mine alone, I realized.

At that moment I felt as light as I do when I am writing longhand on unruled paper, focusing only on the sentence, unburdened by any need for beginning or closure; and like the tense rhythm of a pencil's lead on paper, the sounds of people walking on the boulevard and the occasional horn of a vehicle and the low grumble of motorbikes right now had a positive effect on me.

Nothing would change in the world of action, I knew. In an hour or so I would enter Soi6 and fuck a new whore. I would have some beer before and after that. Then I would walk past Marie Bar Beer, just to check if Noon was there. If I found her, I would share a drink with her, maybe have a photo of us taken. I would then try to gift her that photo. I would spend the whole day with her. After that I would say goodbye and probably have a heavy Thai dinner all by myself. Or maybe I would invite Noon to dinner. I would then go back to my room to let the night glide by. Or maybe I would invite Noon to my room as well, not for anything more than a short round of beers …

(36)

But it rained. Fat droplets fell on my face as I exited the place where I had gone in for some foot reflexology. Grey clouds grumbled every now and then. I rushed toward Soi6, trying to move under the awnings of the various cafes and bars as much as I could. I looked down when I crossed the joint where the girl I had fucked twice in the last two days might have been available. I looked down also before the joint where the old woman could have been. I entered a lounge bar at the far end of Soi6, the one close to Marie Bar Beer. Wet as I was from the rain,

I nevertheless sat on an imitation-leather couch and ordered a Singha. Almost immediately, a fair Thai girl approached me, and even before she could say a word I said yes aloud. I left my beer behind and followed her to a room upstairs. She gave me the towel, and I started using it to dry myself, but then she hinted toward the bathroom and I remembered that I had to in fact take a shower. After the showers, we started doing what we were supposed to do. She had some crumpled skin on her lower belly, like a dried mango, and it was clear that she had had a child not too long back. This fact unnerved me once again, and because of this, or perhaps because of a combination of various things—the rain, the foot reflexology, my mindset or the adequate sexual activity lately—I just could not come. We tried for long, my exertions in the heightened humidity of the room had me soaked in sweat, and there came a point when I just gave up. The woman took it as an affront. Maybe she thought that if I was not satisfied I would not pay. To dispel her fear I told her that it was okay, that it was not her fault, and that I would pay her the price nevertheless. But she was unwilling to accept this settlement. She wanted me to come, and her insistence seemed to be a matter of adhering to some hidden Pattaya code that mandated a client's satisfaction even if the client had no energy for such a thing. It was a frustrating situation, maybe a bit funny too, for I knew that sex with her could not make me come. The only way it could happen was if I did it by myself, though that too could take a long time. But she insisted. And so I started stroking myself back into excitement, with her by my side, kissing me intently and rubbing my chest. I contracted all my muscles and pushed, and after some minutes I did come, though it happened only after I had closed my eyes and imagined that the whore was in love with me.

When I exited the bar the rain had become lighter. The air was filled with a strange youthful quality and also some melancholy, both of which I inhaled with every breath. It became necessary that I go to a place that I was familiar with. I walked to Marie Bar Beer. The place was empty save the woman whose job it was to manage the cash counter. I sat down and ordered a coffee, and the woman looked at me smilingly. 'Coffee?' she asked, as if allowing me the time to rethink what I wanted. After some time, after she cleaned the bar top and the bottles and washed a few of the glasses, she asked if she could join me. She poured herself a whiskey. 'Noon hap to work, you understand, right?' she asked.

That she mentioned Noon without my having asked her, that she both explained to me that Noon had to work and cared if I understood that fact, that Noon had told her coworkers at the bar about me—all of this made me smile. I rejected my coffee and ordered a whiskey, at which this lean woman of deep wrinkles and unruly hair gave me an approving wink. I realized that I could ask questions about Noon and that she would be happy to answer.

'Was Noon a nurse before she came to Pattaya?' I asked.

'Yes,' the woman said. 'Bangkok. She new in Pattaya.'

'Why did she have to come here then?'

'She hap to make more money, no? She hap trouble.'

'Okay.'

Just then the broad broad emerged from behind the bar. She looked at me and grinned, and this time I did not find anything wrong with that grin. I think I grinned back, even raised my glass to further acknowledge her presence. She came up to us and asked me if I would buy her a drink. I bought her one, after which she told me her name, which I cannot of course recollect.

'You come for Noon?' the broad broad asked me.

'Ye-yes,' I answered. I felt a certain fear in certifying that I had come for a specific girl, for Noon; it was as if I were exposing a weakness.

'She get married to Korean man,' the broad broad

said. The cashier woman immediately slapped her on the arm. It was clearly something that could not be revealed, or could not be revealed to me.

The shock of it did not hit me immediately. My first thought was that the man I had mistook as Japanese was in fact Korean. But then the word 'marriage' was heeded in my mind, and at once I was overtaken by an immense confusion that took me violently off guard. My eyes must have betrayed me, for the cashier woman placed her hand upon mine and said, 'She hap to work.'

Hearing this I could feel my own pulse quickening. What work demanded marriage? I thought, stupidly. The answer was of course too clear. But then there were other questions in my head: Why had Noon talked about me? What had she said? Had she decided to marry this Korean man only yesterday? Was it really going to be a marriage? et cetera. But as the rage subsided in silence and the lights in the street adjoining Marie Bar Beer slowly came into their own, I knew that what concerned me most was not how Noon had felt for me or how Noon had agreed to marry the Korean man. It was, strangely, the question of her happiness. I wanted to know if I had made her happy, if the Korean man had made her happy, if marriage with the Korean man would make her happy; I wanted to know the amount of sadness she had at this very instant and whether she was moving to a life of more happiness.

(37)

This time, as you can see, I took pause at happiness.

(38)

I drank more at Marie Bar Beer as the night thickened and the women who worked there joined in and showered the other customers with their attention. Perhaps they were aware too that I would reserve my interest, at least at Marie Bar Beer, only to Noon. For company, I had the cashier lady who continued to sit opposite me and take sips of whatever drink it was that she was having. She was also reading a little book, and when I asked her what it was she passed it to me. It had for cover a cartoon of a Pattaya girl in a go-go costume. It was titled 'Pattaya Bar Girl Handbook' and had no more than fifty tiny pages, each of which contained sentences in Thai and their translation in English. I skimmed through the book, and I saw *Sir, your penis is too big for me … Sir, I do not suck cock … Sir, I will not do anal sex*, et cetera. The discovery of this booklet meant that there should be other such little things to be discovered in Pattaya, and that I, by whoring and getting massaged and worrying about the neon lights, hadn't really looked at, or into, Pattaya; I hadn't really tried to discover what the prostitutes did to be who they were. Where the gaudy dresses were made, what cosmetic brands were preferred, where did these women really live—these would be interesting bits to know. Whenever my Pattaya trip turned into a written story, a turning that I knew I would ensure, it could benefit from these additional details. These would endow my story with some journalistic authority if not anything else.

It was while thinking of this, of little discoveries and the great time they require that I hit upon the realization that it was my last night in Pattaya. It disconcerted me, and not without ill-feeling did I think that tomorrow would bring the return to Mumbai. To think that Pattaya was almost over filled me with a kind of dread, because I knew that now I would be left to think about whether Pattaya did or did not give me what I had come here for. At that point I felt that the story had not ended; or perhaps, because I was aware, and am aware, that stories in real life do not seek an inflection for an end, that in fact real life is constantly fizzling out and has no stories to talk about, I was disappointed with the ending that was staring down my tired face: there was loud music; there was the lust of the customers and the pliant touches of the dolled-up girls; there was the cashier lady sitting opposite me and reading a booklet of smut education; there were taxis on the road carrying fat clients and their thin girls; there were tourists crowding the footpaths … and there was rain, lots and lots of it, again.

(39)

To end it right here is a big temptation, for the rest of the night is something that I have not made sense of completely. It might just be too banal. There are occasions when I consider it as the stuff of soap operas, sentimental tosh of the kind that this story has already suffered a lot from. At other times, I think of that night's subsequent events as the best end—even better than what fiction could provide—to my story of Pattaya. I think it is an end that seems quite like the middle, yet carries the weight of intention that an end should have. As you must have guessed, it involves Noon. But please don't expect too much. It is not that I come out of the end understanding Noon any better; she remains as unknowable as in the middle of the story. It is also not that I come out of the end with any shred of dignity; I remain as naked as in the middle of the story. What happens—and this is my best explanation for it—is that Noon's unknowability and my nakedness shed their malaise.

(40)

The broad broad and the cashier lady looked toward the road and shrieked in joy. I looked up sluggishly from my drink. Noon had arrived on the back of a motorbike taxi. She was in a yellow raincoat, and for a moment she looked to me like a schoolgirl returning from a late evening class. While she paid the bike rider, and as my excitement grew, I caught the cashier lady looking at me with a wistful smile. I gathered that she and the broad broad were happy not because of seeing Noon, which is something they did every day, but because they expected good things out of the meeting between me and Noon, which was, perhaps, a kind of meeting they did not see that often.

Noon waved at me and smiled. I think I smiled back. Then she came close to me and started taking off her raincoat, but because our gazes were locked and because she was a bit too eager to take the raincoat off, she couldn't manage to do it as swiftly as she wanted to. We laughed together, probably in the shared knowledge that meeting me had made Noon visibly happy, that she didn't want to waste a minute doing little things, that she was excited enough to want to tear out of the raincoat. My inhibitions and questions about her vanished into thin air.

I helped her with the raincoat the second time. 'Thank you,' Noon said.

I noticed then the rather gaudy party dress that Noon was in, a dress that began too late and ended too soon, and the meaning of the dress disturbed me.

Noon sat on the stool next to mine. 'You hap fun in Pattaya?' she asked.

'No,' I said.

'NO!?' she laughed at that.

'No. Because I didn't see you a second time.'

'I hap to work.'

'Are you coming back from a party?'

Noon didn't understand my question. So I repeated it, but this time I replaced the word 'party' with 'customer'.

'Yes,' she answered.

At that point the cashier lady came in and talked to Noon in Thai. It was obvious that I was a part of their conversation. Suddenly Noon turned to me and said, 'You here for four hours?'

'Yes,' I said.

'For me?'

'Yes, to meet you.'

'But why?'

The cashier lady excused herself, letting us have the privacy to have a little argument.

'Because I wanted to see you before I left,' I said. 'I am leaving tomorrow.'

'You go tomorrow? India?'

'Yes.'

'When you come back?'

'I don't know.'

Noon sighed and turned, staring at something distant. To be, she had to delete her past, and she had to let go of that bothersome idea of the future. This was what the world demanded of her. Whatever her story was, it was a story more painful than mine. And there was no Pattaya for her to go to. For she was already in real Pattaya, where pains like hers were massacred each day. Softly I took her arm and pulled her toward me. Her beautiful face, blackened by the smudged eyeliner, her eyelashes dabbed in tears. 'You marry Korean man?' I asked. My question startled her. She gave out a sob, implored me with her eyes to talk about something else. And then she burst out crying. She hid her face with her hands, hid it so tightly that I could not make her show it for a while. Embarrassed, I looked around. The broad broad was sipping her whiskey solemnly, with a stern hopelessness on her face that I could not bear more than one glance of. The cashier lady was looking at us and chewing her nails. The other women and their customers, unmindful of us, were doing what they were wont to do. Then Noon showed her face, taut and expressionless. What was shame had mutated into strength. I repeated my question, needlessly, but my voice was now bottomless. Noon clasped my hands tightly. 'Yes, I marry Korean man,' she said.

There was a pause. I couldn't think of what to say.

'I like you very much,' Noon said.

'Me too.'

'I go to Seoul in one week. Korean man hap money.'

'Great.'

'You hap fun in Pattaya?'

'Yes, I had fun.'

'I'm sorry I make bad your vacation.'

'No, don't be sorry.'

'You should go. You should go to more bar.'

'Why?'

'Hap fun, please. Please go. Tomorrow you go to India. So hap fun tonight, please.' Noon pushed me and turned away, exaggeratedly. She didn't really want me to go.

'I want to be here with you,' I said.

'But I hap to go. I hap to change my dress and then I hap to go.'

'To the Korean man?'

'Yes.'

'How much time do you have?'

'Eh?'

'What time do you have to leave?'

'In … in one.'

'Hour?'

'Yes.'

'Do you want a drink?'

'Okay. Beer?'

I ordered beers for us both. The cashier lady brought them. Noon took out an iPhone from her little purse and showed it to her. They talked in hurried Thai. I understood that the phone was a gift from Noon's fiancé. Then Noon wiggled the fingers on her right hand, one of which was wearing a rather spectacular ring. I found this exhibitionism vulgar, but as soon as the cashier lady left us, Noon's expressions took a grim air.

'He pay twenty thousand baht for me. And he gibme iPhone and ring,' she said.

I nodded. There couldn't be any exhibitionism. Everything was a coping mechanism.

'I go to Seoul,' she said.

'Yes, Noon. You will go to Seoul.'

'And you to go to India.'

'Yes. I will go to India.'

With eyes locked into each other's we talked in short sentences that were easier to understand. After a while Noon said that she had to change her dress, and went behind the bar. As soon as she left, the cashier lady came up to me. 'I want to tell you something,' she whispered.

'Hmm.'

'The Korean man come here daily. He like Noon. But Noon no like him. You first customer for Noon. But Korean man hap more money. You understand? She hap to work.'

'But why does she have to marry him?' I asked. 'He only wants her for the sex, no?'

'Do you hap money?'

I only had silence as a reply.

Noon returned. She had put on the same clothes that I had seen on her the first time: the pink top, the black jeans, the denim jacket. She took a cigarette out of her purse and lit it. The cash lady went back to mending the counter.

'What she tell you?' Noon said.

'Nothing.'

The rain intensified, and the loud pattering sound subsumed the sound of music from the bars. Noon looked worried; she told me that she had to leave in some time. I asked her to pass the cigarette to me. She did. I caressed her cheeks as I smoked and she looked back at me blankly. Then I crushed the cigarette in an ashtray and tried to kiss her on the lips. She didn't let me, turning a cheek toward me instead. Then she put her hands on my shoulders and made to hug me. It was an awkward position, the two of us seated on high stools and hugging.

'I want you to hap fun,' Noon said into my ear, still holding me.

'What fun?'

'I want you to hap lady tonight.'

'Really!' I said, breaking the hug. Getting a lady for the night was the last thing on my mind.

'Yes.'

'But I want you,' I blurted out.

'I hap to go.'

'I know,' I said loudly. There was the sound of a million rain drops hitting the asphalt.

'You know the song?' Noon said.

I tried to listen. A faint beat was discernible; it was something familiar, from a Bollywood movie.

'It's Hindi song. Dhoom Dhoom. Tata Young … Thai singer. She sing this song.' Noon tried to dance a bit without getting off her stool.

'I don't want you to marry the Korean man,' I said.

She stopped dancing. 'I hap to.'

That was the moment. It was then that I could have decided to use my money, to buy her and bring her to India with me and wed her and love her. I did consider all this, only to quickly concede defeat to the Korean man's decisiveness. But being indecisive did not mean that my feelings were ambiguous. I was in the middle of a possibility of love, a possibility that wanted more but could be content with being just what it was. I felt no compulsions; I didn't want anything more to happen than what was already happening. And maybe it was the same for Noon, she who looked into my eyes for distended minutes, she who locked her fingers in mine, she who lit a cigarette for me, she who didn't want to leave me but knew that she should and would.

'I like you very much.'

'Me too.'

'If Korean man no good, I come back to Pattaya. In December. You come to Pattaya in December?'

'I will come to Pattaya in December,' I said. 'I promise.'

The promise did something to her, something enormous for the dimensions of her heart. She got up from the stool and dragged me outside, to the street, where the rain didn't waste even a second in drenching us.

(It is what happened next that had made me reluctant about writing any of this.)

We kissed. But it was not a mere kiss. It took place on the middle of road, under a downpour. The taxi drivers grew delirious with rage for having to wait for it to end. It was, in fact, not a single kiss but a flurry of kisses, and in-between Noon held my head in her hands and shouted the words 'I want you to hap fun.' We kissed not like two people in love, but like two people in love with the possibility of love, with the affirmation that it could happen with us too, for us too, by us too, that we could hold the other person and make a promise that we would keep no matter what, no matter how impossible our lives had turned the idea of our being together, and no matter how hard our worlds would still try to make us renege on that promise. And it didn't just *end.* Noon took my hand as we got abuses from folks on the road and cheers from the ladies inside Marie Bar Beer. She led me through Second Road for some distance, and then we turned to a street that I hadn't been to before. I asked her where she was taking me. She repeated that she wanted me to have fun. There were some bars on this street. Noon took me inside one called 'Capital Bar'.

'The most beautiful lady in Pattaya,' Noon said. 'My friend. She work here. I want you to take her tonight.'

It was dark and cramped inside. There was a narrow stage surrounded by narrow stools and tables. Noon waved to a costumed girl who was contorted around a steel pole on the stage. The bar was almost empty, possibly because of the heavy rain, so the costumed girl didn't have any problem stopping her act and coming over to us.

Noon introduced the girl as Agun. Agun had facial features that were not as Thai as other women in Pattaya. She seemed to have a Western streak in her blood. In sheer sexiness, she beat Noon hands down, especially in the kind of sexiness valued in the Pattaya business. She was a hardcore business girl.

'Agun best girl in Pattaya,' Noon said. 'She my friend. You enjoy with her, okay?'

'But what about you?' I asked Noon.

'Now I hap to go to Korean man.'

Next to us, Agun put on her clothes swiftly. Then she tugged me on the elbow and gave me a happy grin. She was beautiful. I looked at Noon, her eyes. 'I come in December,' I said.

'I know you come. But maybe I no come.' Noon said. Her clothes were dripping and it occurred to me that the Korean man might not like that. But there was no point thinking about that.

'It's okay,' I said. 'I will wait for one week. From Christmas to New Year's.'

'Okay,' she said, holding my hands with that strange longing that assails one just before saying goodbye. We hugged. Then all three of us moved outside, in the rain. Noon kissed me on the lips again.

'I love you,' she said, almost perfunctorily. I felt compelled to say the same, but didn't. 'Next time you tell new soldier story, okay?' she said then, and it was on hearing this that I, I who considered himself broken enough, broke again.

Noon ran into the street, to be made invisible by the heavy raindrops. I kept staring at the watery streets and the spread of neon on them. 'You beautiful man,' Agun said after some seconds, probably after she realized that she had to interject, that otherwise I would be staring at that blank static of rain for a long time.

(41)

When your salvation depends on love, you don't waste any time. It can brew immediately after the first meeting; it can culminate as soon as the second one. These, and other such, were my thoughts inside the taxi that Agun and I had hailed to take us to my hotel room. As the rain fell heavily on the car's windows, the neon city of Pattaya transformed into a mellow image of itself. Its colours spread and gained benevolence.

I didn't know the import of Noon's kisses, the meaning of her 'I love you'. I didn't know if I was in love with her. But an enormous kindness had overtaken me, a wellness of being, as if some nourishment long sought had been finally had. Did that mean that I would not take pleasure in the prostitute next to me? No. Agun was a gift from Noon. I had accepted Noon's injunction to enjoy with Agun, and in the taxi ride I internalized this fact whole heartedly. Perhaps I was justifying my immorality. I didn't know if I was supposed to pay Agun or not, but I knew that my time with her would be great and that it would—in a convoluted way—give meaning to my image of Noon. I was strangely comfortable with her, was able to converse with her like I would with any woman in Mumbai (she spoke English well). It was as if she too had become softer in the rain, as if she too had been washed clean of all the insinuations and accents and connotations of Pattaya, and for a while it seemed that the two of us held a higher ground and could see why all of this—the city of Pattaya, its grey clouds, its silver linings, its base humanity, its rare human connections—was a sort of world too.

That night, I had sex with Agun thrice, and I enjoyed it immensely each time. She was almost entrepreneurial in bed. The only blemish on her body was the long scars just below her breasts. 'I had fake breasts once,' she told me. I paid her handsomely, at a rate higher than any that I had accepted in Pattaya, not minding that at all. I offered to let her sleep in my bed, but she declined and left the room. This gave me time to pack my things, to smoke a cigarette looking at the P A T T A Y A sign one last time. It was probably two in the morning. The rain had lessened to a negligible drizzle. The streets were still quiet and one could hear the sea waves hit the little beach periodically. I finished my cigarette and turned, and my gaze fell on Anne-Marie's photograph stuck on the mirror. I instinctively took it off and tore it, feeling nothing, or feeling very little. When I blew the dead parts out of the window, the words of the Japanese geisha Kimiko came back to me. And I had a silly wish: that Noon should come to the hotel tomorrow and see the torn bits. Knowing it to be impossible, I closed my window and started reading.

Acknowledgements

I thank my first readers—Mohit Parikh, Apoorv Vyas, Ujjwal Agarwal, and Mihir Vatsa. I thank Manasi Subramaniam, my editor at HarperCollins. I thank Alexandra Le Trionnaire, for letting me break the promise that I would dedicate all my books to her. I thank Satyavir chacha, whose passion for books I inherited, if only in part. I thank my wife who was courageous enough to love me and marry me after reading the novel in its raw form. I thank my late father: the memory of him struggling with one of my published stories late at night, despite his patchy English, has inspired me many times. I thank my mother, who is very much in the habit of asking me, every other day, to be 'awesome'. I thank my brother, conversations with whom always remind me of my ten-year-younger self.

Parts of this novel appeared as short stories in forms vastly different from the current ones in various literary magazines around the world. The first chapter appeared as 'The Other Room' in *One Throne*

Magazine, run by the indomitable George Filipovic; the second chapter appeared in *The Atticus Review*; the third chapter in *Out of Print magazine*, perhaps the best space for short stories in India, run by Indira Chandrasekhar. The two chapters in the second part were both published in the *Burrow Press Review*, then edited by Hunter Choate and Ryan Rivas. The first, published as 'The Bachelor', was also nominated for the Pushcart Prize.

About the Author

Tanuj Solanki lives in Mumbai. His short fiction has appeared in the *Caravan*, *DNA*, *Hindu Business Line*, *Out of Print* and numerous other publications. He's a Pushcart nominee and a two-time runner-up in the DNA-Out of Print short fiction contest. He is also the founder of the *Bombay Literary Magazine*. His second book, a collection of short stories, is due in 2017.